I0573357

Surge

Caroline Carter

CRIMSON
ROMANCE
F+W Media, Inc.

Published by
Crimson Romance
an imprint of F+W Media, Inc.
10151 Carver Road, Suite 200
Blue Ash, Ohio 45242

www.crimsonromance.com

Copyright © 2013 by Caroline Carter

ISBN 10: 1-4405-6475-2
ISBN 13: 978-1-4405-6475-8
eISBN 10: 1-4405-6476-0
eISBN 13: 978-1-4405-6476-5

This is a work of fiction. Names, characters, corporations, institutions, organizations, events, or locales in this novel are either the product of the author's imagination or, if real, used fictitiously. The resemblance of any character to actual persons (living or dead) is entirely coincidental.

Chapter 1

Lara stretched each muscle in her body and exhaled slowly and fully. *Come on brain…fire up,* she urged herself silently. Time to pull herself together.

It was the start of second semester at Melbourne University's law school, and Lara was struggling to adjust to her recent change in environment, from the wild ocean beaches of Anglesea where she'd spent the holiday period, to this airless and timeless lecture theatre. All around her, the twenty or so other students who'd achieved strong first-term results in criminal law lounged on the hard wooden benches, getting out their notebooks or setting up their laptops. Sitting up straighter in her seat, she sighed and willed her mind and spirit to join her body in the room.

But just as the class became focused and the tutor, Mrs. James, rose to scrawl notes on the whiteboard behind her, Lara's attention was caught by a silent stirring of air as the door re-opened to admit someone new at the last minute. A guy, dressed in jeans and a faded black t-shirt that fitted closely around his slim body. He carried an old bomber jacket in one hand and the relevant textbook and a notepad in the other. A new student. A different kind of student. With tousled brown hair that fell across one side of his face and piercing blue eyes that darted around the room in an instant stock-take, he looked tougher, more masculine than the brainiacs and private school boys around him. No guessing what sort of person he'd be with those looks though, Lara thought distractedly. Definitely not someone from her world.

"Ah, you must be Mr. Black, transferred from Sydney," said Mrs. James, registering his arrival and bending over the enrollment list. A sea of faces turned to the stranger, and an almost imperceptible murmur passed around the room, followed by a stifled giggle from two girls sitting at the front. "Please take a seat wherever you like. We were just about to get stuck into the niceties of manslaughter." She smiled ironically.

He grinned in return, and with a gravelly "thanks," moved to a seat directly across the other side of the wide U-shaped seating arrangement from Lara. She watched vaguely as he settled in and sorted through the paperwork he'd been handed. Then she returned her full attention to the front of the room as the class resumed.

At one point, "Mr. Black" answered one of Mrs. James's questions about a landmark case clearly and succinctly. Lara glanced involuntarily across at him as the discussion moved on, and was taken aback to find him looking straight back at her. She scowled and looked away, hating the feeling of being watched. *No attention required over here, thanks Mister.* She passed the rest of the class with her gaze focused deliberately on the tutor.

When the ninety minutes of class was up and they'd been assigned a decent volume of reading material for the next tutorial, Lara slung the strap of her shoulder bag across her body and followed the others out of the room. The new mystery man was standing just outside the doorway, so that she almost had to brush against him as she exited. Her senses were assaulted by a distinctive musky, masculine scent as she moved past him, vaguely aware that two girls from the front row, Sally and Kristen, were introducing themselves to him with big smiles and asking his name.

"Marcus," came his audible reply, before Lara disappeared through the cloisters of the old building and headed to the library. Marcus. Marcus Black. Whatever.

Chapter 2

On Wednesday morning, Lara made two cappuccinos—thanks to her one indulgence, an espresso machine—and went next door. She lived in the historic suburb of Carlton in a converted first-floor bedsitter—the typical student's existence. The residence next door, a mirror image of her own, was occupied by Daniel, an extroverted gay guy with whom Lara shared a warm friendship. They'd started this mid-week ritual about a year earlier, and got together without fail throughout each term to analyze human nature, discuss potential romantic interests and failed dates (him), and describe the ups and downs of university life (her), which Daniel found fascinating, given that he hadn't even finished school.

This morning, Daniel was dressed in tight black pants and a loud '70s paisley shirt he'd undoubtedly picked up at his favorite thrift shop. After giving Lara a giant bear hug and her holiday mail, he launched straight into all of his news about the café/bar where he worked, focusing in particular on the arrival of a new customer—a handsome young businessman who was coming in almost daily and who seemed to be lingering more and more often…

After a short while though, he ceased his musings and turned to Lara.

"Well, that's enough about me and my little world. What's going on with you, genius? How was the beach? How is that great institution of higher learning up the road treating you?"

She gave him a quick summary of her time away: her surfing escapades, walks on the back beach, and cozy nights by the fire. He raised an eyebrow at a couple of her descriptions, silently signifying his views on her "wholesome" outdoor activities. Smiling to herself, Lara moved swiftly to university talk, describing a student rally that was being organized on campus to protest the recent rise in fees, while Daniel listened with wide eyes. This was more his style! Then, just as their breakfast was coming to a close, he started down a line of questioning that always got a little under her skin.

"And, honey, I don't suppose I even need to ask whether any interesting man has entered the scene? You're just going to give me the stock standard 'no comment, not interested,' aren't you?" asked Daniel. "*Such* a waste for mainstream mankind, you know."

Daniel knew just how non-existent Lara's love life was and how inexperienced she was with the opposite sex, and he was constantly trying to encourage her to change that sorry state of affairs. Usually she had nothing to offer him in reply, but this time she must have hesitated for a nanosecond—just enough time for Daniel to hone in like a bloodhound. He leaned forward and peered into her eyes.

"Good God, girl, something's happened, hasn't it? Don't even try to hide it from me, Lara! Tell me *everything*, this instant! Who's the lucky man?"

"No, no, you've got it all wrong," she insisted with a laugh, having to raise her voice over the top of his to stop his runaway thoughts. "There's no man! I was just thinking that there was someone 'interesting' who's started classes with me…just interesting as in 'different.' He looks more like he belongs on a billboard selling some hip new product than in a law lecture, that's all," she explained. "So, of course, every girl in the faculty is talking about him."

"Including you, it seems," Daniel observed pointedly.

"Sorry to disappoint, but he's not my type, Daniel."

"I'd love to know exactly what *is* your type, girl." Daniel sighed. "It's very elusive."

She smiled in the face of his frustration. "Well, whatever it may be, it sure isn't physical perfection. I couldn't handle the arrogance."

"That's presumptuous."

"Wherever there's smoke, on the other hand…"

"Hmmm. You could do with a bit of fire in your life, if you ask me. We might have to work on this one. Things could develop, you know, if you play your cards right and work on your sex appeal," said Daniel with a scheming look in his eye. "The raw material's there, all right; it can just be a bit buried at times…oh, honey, I've made you blush! Now you'll definitely have to keep me posted about this guy. I've got a feeling about him."

"All right, nosey." She laughed again. "But you're wrong, you know. I haven't even spoken to him, and I don't intend to. I'm not in town to pick up a man, Daniel, and even if I was, he's way out of my league. Don't be so desperate on my behalf!"

Daniel just waggled his eyebrows knowingly in response, which resulted in a gentle whack across his shoulder before they parted for the day.

*

Once she'd made her way into the large lecture theatre for the torts class an hour later, Lara took her usual seat toward the back of the room. Looking around, she saw Marcus sitting across from her and down a couple of rows, running his hand through his hair as he sorted through his books. Once again, although just dressed in an old t-shirt and faded jeans, he could have leapt out of a magazine ad, with his athletic build and air of style and confidence.

Sally and Kristen had apparently noticed him too, as they moved quickly over to sit at the empty bench beside him. A couple of their friends joined them as well, the guys shaking Marcus's hand and making introductions. It looked as if he had fallen into the most social group in the faculty without even trying, Lara thought wryly. That's what those looks could do for you. What must it be like to live such a charmed life?

It had taken her weeks just to talk to another soul when she'd started at this giant campus. No wonder the best-looking people were usually the most boring and smug—there was no need to develop a whole heap of character if you could attract an eager crowd regardless.

Among the students in the room sat Lara's two friends. While she'd generally been a loner during her first year on campus, she'd slowly become close to this unusual pair. The three of them were distinctive in that they weren't the stereotype second or third generation law students racing to earn their first million, but that was really where the similarities ended. Kate, strong and proud, who had used her razor-sharp mind to top the state's final school exams and who was fascinated by all aspects of the law, was destined to become a judge. And Pete, disheveled and disorganized, was passionate about human rights law and even more so about live music and his pub band, Burst. Although Lara still often sat alone in lectures for concentration purposes, the eclectic threesome regularly hung out together for a catch-up and some laughs, gossip, and legal-speak. And, because of their characters and their differences, there was never a dull moment.

As the class got underway and everyone got busy taking notes on the critical topic of negligence, Lara continued to glance curiously over to where Marcus sat, still pondering the marked differences in people's university experiences. After a while, she realized two things: Firstly, he wasn't taking any more notes than she was. And secondly, he seemed to be watching someone intently toward the front of the room, near to where Pete sat with Kate, rather than absorbing the content of the lecture. She frowned as she stared at his profile, wondering what had caught his attention.

Just then though, he must have sensed her stare, as he turned his head quickly and looked directly into her eyes. Their gazes held for a second before he turned away with the subtlest of smiles, causing her to flinch in embarrassment. Great, she groaned inwardly. No doubt he thought she had just signed up as the latest member of his fan club, an observation that couldn't have been further from the truth.

After two hours, the class was dismissed and the crowd began to disperse. Lara waved at Kate, pointing toward the library where she had decided to keep to herself and photocopy some reference material. Seeing Marcus and Co. standing nearby, she moved away behind some bodies and turned hurriedly into the entrance of the quiet law quadrangle. But after only a few steps, she tripped over the quad's uneven paving stones, dropping her water bottle and course notes as she protected herself from the fall.

Groaning in annoyance, she leaned over to pick up the fallen items, only to have the flap of her bag open so that more items spilled out onto the ground.

"Damn!" she exclaimed, hoping that nobody had witnessed her complete lack of poise. Turning around then, she was mortified to lay eyes on the very person she least wanted to see, standing only meters away and watching her with crossed arms, openly amused at her irritated expression. Marcus Black. Why on earth had he come this way? Her eyes flashed at him and she flicked her dark hair back angrily before whirling around to reclaim her stray possessions, deliberately ignoring him and praying he'd get the message and just go away. But a few seconds later, she was agonizingly aware that he was leaning down next to her, picking up her keys and lip balm. Then, as they stood back up together, she held out her hand, careful not to touch his as he returned her things in silence.

When she'd finally packed everything safely away, Lara took a steadying breath and looked up at her helper. The plan was to utter a dignified "thanks," but the plan came unstuck. Lara wasn't sure whether it was the remaining laughter in his eyes, the enticing potency of his scent, or the fact that she was in the presence of the most beautiful person she'd ever seen. But whatever the reason, she suddenly felt utterly insecure and disorientated, and found that she could barely breathe. Then instinct took over, and she turned and walked quickly away without saying a word.

"Wait, please!" he called to her back, but Lara only walked faster. She knew he must be thinking that she was the rudest person alive and that she'd probably cringe about it later, but right then she didn't care—she just wanted out.

Around the corner and out of the quadrangle, she bolted as fast as she could to the library, and then to her labor law class, keeping a very low profile for the rest of the unproductive day.

*

When she woke the next day, Lara remembered her immature response to Marcus's assistance, and crushed her pillow down onto her face with a grimace. What on earth had gotten into her? Since when had anyone made her so nervous or made her doubt herself like that…and just because of his looks! How truly tragic her behavior had been. She went into the bathroom and took a good look at herself in the mirror. A slim, fit young woman stared back at her with fierce dark eyes, a capable woman with enough life experience to handle anyone and anything. Except an intoxicating demi-god, apparently.

Determined to get back on the front foot, Lara arrived at the morning's criminal law class a few minutes early, with her head held high. Sliding into a vacant seat at the back of the room, she pulled out her notepad and began doodling idly while the conversation buzzed around her.

Then, shortly before Mrs. James commenced the tutorial, she felt rather than saw someone sink into the seat beside her. A moment later, the unmistakable scent hit her, and the hairs rose on the back of her neck. Slowly and deliberately, she took a deep breath before forcing herself to turn her gaze toward Marcus. She found that he was already looking at her, but without the mockery she'd expected after the previous day's performance. Instead, his look was guarded.

"Hi again, stranger," he said simply, after a pause. She gave him a half-smile, the best greeting she could offer with her heart hammering in her chest. So much for self-confidence. She was off-balance again already.

"Do I at least get a name?" he prodded, alerting her to her silence. She cleared her throat.

"Lara. It's Lara," she managed.

"Lara," he repeated, nodding slightly. "That fits. Well, I'm Marcus. And it's nice to meet you, Lara. Better late than never, I guess." With that, he gave her a wry smile and held out his hand. Taken aback, she felt obliged to meet his grasp, but instantly regretted the move when her body reacted to the contact with an involuntary shiver. She pulled abruptly out of the handshake as if she'd received a shock, hoping he hadn't noticed. Unfortunately, though, it seemed that he had.

"Don't like me very much, do you?" he observed.

"What? No, that's not it," she replied, embarrassed.

"Then what is it?" he asked, seemingly genuinely confused. "Because it's something."

But she could only blush and shake her head in response, incapable of explaining something she didn't really understand herself. At her prolonged silence, he leaned back in his chair and sighed.

"All right, then. Some other time, maybe," he finished quietly for both of them, before turning to face the front of the room as the class began.

Lara moved her seat slightly away from Marcus's, hoping that a bit of extra distance would protect her from his magnetic pull, and would help her to concentrate. It didn't work. She sat restlessly for the entire period, hyper-aware of his every move and sound at her side and desperate to escape the tension that had invaded her entire body in his presence. He certainly didn't seem similarly affected, leaning back casually in his chair and following the group discussion. Sitting right next to him was not an option for the future, Lara realized. She was acting like a movie star groupie, instead of her usual together self.

The minute the class ended, before Marcus could say another word to her, Lara grabbed her bag and hurried out the door, gratefully releasing her tightened muscles as she went. She ducked quickly around the back of the building and made her escape.

Chapter 3

The following morning, Lara felt a true lightening of her spirits. She was going home! Armed with a small backpack, she headed directly from uni toward the middle of the city with wings on her heels, to take a train south to the satellite city of Geelong, and a connecting bus that wound along the coastal road to the town of Anglesea.

The bus dropped her at the quiet end of town, and she stood for a minute breathing in the salt air and allowing her body to adapt to its changed surroundings before hitching up her backpack and setting off down the hill to the narrow dirt road that she knew like the back of her hand. At the end of it, hidden behind an old picket fence and a busy landscape of native flora lay the pale weatherboard cottage she loved like no other place. Almost skipping down the driveway, she burst through the kitchen door, which, as always, was unlocked.

"Gran!" she called out, throwing her bag on the kitchen table. "I'm home!" Before anything else could happen though, she heard the scamper of giant paws on floorboards as a suddenly alert black Labrador came skidding around the corner from the living room, ears pricked and tongue lolling, and bowled directly into her. "Hiya, Chief." She laughed, crouching down on one knee to give her dog a giant bear hug, as excited to see him as he was to see her.

"Lara, my dear," said the elderly lady who'd just entered the room and was approaching her with a smile, arms outstretched. They held each other in a tight embrace for several seconds before stepping back. "You've arrived just at low tide…I was about to take Chief for his beach walk. Why don't we go together? I can't wait to hear all of your Melbourne news!"

Their reunion taking this familiar form, the two of them picked up as if they'd never left off, and Lara slipped immediately back into her comfort zone in the town she'd called home for almost all of her twenty-one years.

*

Lara rose silently at dawn the next morning and headed out the back door with Chief to grab her surfboard and wetsuit from the shed. In a routine as familiar to her as brushing her hair, she squeezed into the tight-fitting suit, waxed her board, and headed for the beach track with a towel over her shoulder. Coming over the rise at the top of the dunes, she was delighted to see a good strong swell. She walked out a short way before plunging into the freezing water, paddling over the waves as she headed out beyond the break, and enjoyed perfect surfing conditions for the next hour before the sea calmed, while Chief faithfully guarded her towel.

Returning home, she spent the better part of the day lounging around in tracksuit pants, sipping cups of tea, and reading the paper, chatting to Gran and taking Chief for a walk. After watching Gran's game shows by the fire in the evening, she fell into bed and was lulled to sleep by the familiar sounds of the sea.

It felt great to be home, and she felt a tightening in her chest as she packed up her city belongings on Sunday evening, preparing to make the trek back to Melbourne. She longed to stay, in so many ways. But duty and the future called, as they inevitably did.

*

On Monday afternoon then, Lara was sprawled on the university lawn in the afternoon sun, with a good novel for company. The book was so totally absorbing, in fact, that it took her a minute to notice that someone had approached, and was standing above her, silhouetted against the blue sky.

"Hi there, Lara. May I join you for a minute?" The husky voice was unmistakable.

Lara sat bolt upright, staring at her visitor with a bemused frown until he cleared his throat meaningfully, alerting her to the growing silence.

"Oh, sorry. Okay, sure," she responded nervously, putting her book away. A moment later, Marcus's lithe frame was sitting on the grass next to her, his backpack thrown to one side.

"I saw you crashed out here, and decided it was the perfect opportunity to clear something up. I've got a question for you, if you don't mind."

"About…?"

"About whether I've said or done something to offend you." He regarded her closely.

"No…of course not…" she stammered in embarrassment.

"So…?" he persisted, one eyebrow raised quizzically. He clearly wasn't going to let this go. Lara shuffled uncomfortably.

"So, you're probably wondering why I've been so unfriendly, when you've been nothing but pleasant and helpful to me," she finished his thought in a halting voice.

"Something like that, yeah," he replied with the shadow of a smile.

"Fair enough, I suppose." She swallowed awkwardly, unnerved at the prospect of having to explain one of the less admirable aspects of her character to this near stranger. Fixing her gaze on a blade of grass in front of her, she paused before choosing her next words with care.

"Look, it's nothing personal, believe me. It's to do with me, actually, not you. I just get—overwhelmed—by some types of people, and don't know how to respond to them. And I guess you're one of those types. But I really haven't meant to be rude or anything. I'm sorry I haven't been more welcoming." She was grateful to have found her voice at last.

"'Some types of people,'" Marcus repeated slowly, an uncertain expression on his face. "I'm not sure what you mean by that, exactly. We barely know each other, after all. But I guess I'm more interested in whether we can move beyond this…impasse. I don't know too many people in Melbourne, and I could really use some friends." At that, Lara felt even worse about her previous rudeness. She knew all too well what it felt like to be an outsider, after all. And just because the guy looked like Adonis didn't mean he didn't deserve some common courtesy.

"Oh, well, when you put it that way…" She looked back up at him with a shy smile. "Let's start over. I know exactly how tough it can be coming to a new city without knowing anyone."

"You do? Where are you from?" he enquired in a more relaxed tone as he settled back on the grass.

"The coast. An hour and a half from Melbourne. Coming to 'the big smoke' was a real shock for a small-town girl like me. How about you? How are you finding it down here?"

"All right, thanks. Still finding my feet a little bit and getting used to the colder weather, but I'm getting there."

They spent a couple of minutes comparing the two cities, agreeing that Sydney was the more beautiful and exciting of the two while Melbourne was more cultured, but disagreeing about which city had the better football code. Lara realized with surprise that she was now enjoying their easy conversation—such a far cry from their former uneasiness.

"So why the big move in the first place?" she eventually asked him. At that question, though, his expression tightened slightly, and he looked away.

"It was just time for a change of scene," he answered elusively. "But I wanted to stick with my legal studies, so I was stoked when this place accepted my transfer application. My grand plan is to be a prosecutor in the next five years. How about you? What's a beach baby doing so far from home?" She noticed that he'd deftly batted the attention away from her own line of questioning.

"I made a promise to my father," was all she replied with a slight frown. Thankfully, he didn't enquire further. He obviously believed, as she did, that everyone was entitled to his or her privacy.

"So, here we both are," he concluded.

"Yep, looks like it," she agreed, and for a long moment they simply looked at each other. Lara could get lost in those blue eyes, given half the chance…

"Well, on that note, time for me to get going and leave you to your book," he said, breaking the spell, and stretching out his arms before reaching for his bag. "So much to do here, always. But thanks for the chat. It's been most…enlightening. And I'm glad we're good now." He smiled.

"Good as gold." She smiled in return.

"So I take it you won't run from me then, the next time I decide to help you out?" His smile had become teasing.

"You have my word."

"And that you might even consider sitting in class with me occasionally?"

"Maybe even that," she agreed.

"Excellent," he said. "Although, on second thoughts, maybe not such a great idea. That perfume you wear is very distracting. What is it, by the way?"

"Just oil of tea rose," she managed to respond in a strangled voice after a brief pause, suddenly uncomfortable once more.

"Tea rose. Hmm. It's amazing, and it suits you," he finished thoughtfully, before rising to his feet. "Right. Well, thanks again. See you in class." And with that, he gave her a final wave, slung his bag over his shoulder, and walked away.

"Yeah, see you," she said quietly to herself as she watched him leave, her thoughts confused now that their meeting had ended.

What was all of this? Why was her heart hammering in her chest, just because he'd sought her out as a friend? And why did she have to feel like she'd been hit by an electrical charge, when he clearly didn't?

Chapter 4

Lara kept her eye out for Marcus over the next couple of days, but he seemed to disappear from the campus immediately after each lecture. She was unnerved at her disappointment, but didn't want to examine it too closely. Her hopes and interest had definitely been raised since their conversation, but where exactly did she think that was going to lead her?

On Thursday, though, Lara sauntered to the cafeteria to have lunch with Kate and Pete, who were already engaged in their usual banter.

"So, troops, who's game for a night out on the town?" Pete was asking. "It's about time you guys came and gave Burst some support. Probably about time you had some real fun too."

"'Fun' comes in all shapes and sizes, Pete," Kate retorted, rolling her eyes. "I can't do anything this weekend, I'm afraid. Going home to see the folks. Maybe next time?"

"I'm out of action for the weekend too, sorry. I'm heading back to the beach," said Lara.

"Yawn," replied Pete, directing a bored expression her way. "Whatever turns you people on, I suppose."

"Speaking of which, have you guys checked out the new male specimen everyone's talking about? Because if not, now's your chance," said Kate, sitting up straighter and inclining her head to the cafeteria entrance. "Mmm, nice, don't you think, Lara? Not too many of that caliber around here."

Lara turned without thinking, and found herself looking straight at Marcus, who had entered the room alone and was unraveling his scarf, turning a number of other heads as he did so. As she gazed at him, her heart rate increased undeniably, and she felt a wave of relief at his return to the campus. For his part, Marcus was seemingly oblivious to the stir he'd created, his eyes busily making a sweep of the room as he searched for someone. Then, as he located Lara, their gazes locked and held, and Lara felt warmth radiate through her entire body. He raised a hand briefly in greeting, the corners of his mouth turning up, before taking a few steps her way.

As he glanced at her companions, though, his half-smile fell and he froze on the spot for a few seconds. A confused expression seemed to flit momentarily across his face, before he took a deep breath and composed himself so completely that the hesitation might never have occurred. Then he continued toward their table, his face blank until he gave another smile—one that didn't quite reach his eyes.

"Hey there, Lara. How's it going, guys?"

Kate stared incredulously at Lara, before turning back to Marcus and smiling warmly in response, greeting him and introducing herself. Pete did the same, standing up and shaking Marcus's hand eagerly.

As Lara murmured her own greeting, Pete dragged a spare chair from the next table and insisted that Marcus join them. The two guys struck up a conversation about Melbourne's nightlife, and Kate took the opportunity to drag Lara to the counter to order another round of coffees.

"You *know* him?" she whispered in amazement the second they were out of the others' earshot.

"No. Well, not really, he's just in my crim class," Lara replied.

"Well, why haven't we already heard about him, girl? You can see from a mile away how amazing he is! And he's remembered your name. Interesting." She gave Lara a gentle prod with her elbow. "Maybe this is one guy you'll actually show some interest in. I certainly would, if I were single!"

Kate had a long-term boyfriend named Matt, who'd recently

launched his career as a promising young architect, and with whom she was hoping to buy a little "renovator's delight" at the end of the year.

"Kate, open your eyes a bit wider…he's completely out of my league! Anyway, if anyone *were* interested in Marcus they'd have to join a long line. He's created a bit of a stir among the girls in criminal law, something I'm sure he's very used to…"

Kate looked appraisingly at Lara. "You think any one of those girls has anything on you? You don't see yourself clearly at all, do you? I guess that's one of the reasons we love you, you crazy tomboy. Well, just don't be too surprised if that guy over there shows you more interest than you're expecting. He'd be mad not to." She led the way back to the table, leaving Lara to hope that her friend wouldn't say anything pushy or embarrassing.

"So, you'll have to come and watch us play, if you're into live music." Pete had obviously become comfortable with Marcus very quickly, and had already worded him up about Burst. "The others are coming to our gig on the first Saturday in August, aren't you girls?" He gave them a half-joking glare. "Why don't you all come as a group?"

"Take it easy, Pete, jeez," Kate replied with an exaggerated sigh. "I'll come along if you stop laying it on so thick! You up for it, Lara?"

"Sure," said Lara, wanting to show her friend some support.

"Okay, I guess it's a date then." After a pause, Marcus smiled. Kate's gaze flickered toward Lara and she gave her a gentle kick on the shin. Pete too was noticeably pleased with the latest addition to his guest list.

"So anyway, where are you living in Melbourne, Marcus, and how long do you plan to stay?" Kate asked him innocently, obviously determined to milk him for personal information on Lara's behalf. He shifted in his seat before responding.

"I've got a small apartment in East Melbourne for the rest of this year, and then I guess I'll see how my study's going. And my finances. I'm not really working right now, apart from a few odd jobs here and there…I'll just have to see how long the savings last. At this stage, I'm not planning any other moves though. Melbourne's a terrific city, and there are plenty of weekend getaway options that aren't too hard to get to."

"Oh God, not another one," Pete groaned. "Why do you guys feel the need to disappear on weekends? Everything a person needs is right here!"

"Don't get me wrong; I like going out in the city," Marcus replied with a grin. "But I also need a regular hit of the great outdoors or I go a bit stir-crazy. So whenever I feel a bit of cabin fever coming on, I go and do a bit of hiking, mountain biking, kayaking…stuff like that. I'm packing a tent and going rock climbing tomorrow."

"Oooh, Lara, a fellow adrenalin junkie!" exclaimed Kate. "Lara's a fanatical surfer, Marcus. You guys should hang out sometime and see which of you can outdo the other in the thrill-seeking department!"

Lara winced at Kate's sledgehammer subtlety. She felt even worse when Marcus, following an initial look of surprise, gave an obviously forced smile in her direction, and dismissed the idea outright.

"Thanks, but I prefer flying solo when it comes to weekend pursuits," he murmured before checking his watch, gathering his belongings and announcing that he had to be off. "Great meeting you all though, and looking forward to your gig, Pete." Marcus wrapped his scarf back around his neck and strode off, without so much as a glance in Lara's direction.

"A good guy, your friend," Pete said to Lara admiringly. Marcus's charisma was clearly not lost on the male of the species any more than the female.

"Not really my friend, I'm thinking," replied Lara, bemused and hurt by Marcus's obvious snub.

"That was so weird," agreed Kate. "I could swear his eyes literally lit up when he first saw you here, but then he seemed really cool just now. I wonder what his story is?"

"Oh, I wouldn't be too concerned if I were you," said Pete. "He couldn't take his eyes off you the whole time you were at the counter, Lara. I think he might like you, but just doesn't want to show it."

Lara stared at Pete in amazement, before shaking her head, determined to brush off the whole encounter. "And you guys mock me for not being interested in dating! Who needs all the uncertainty and game playing? Give me a trusty dog for company over a man any day of the week."

Kate laughed. "We'll see, my friend, we'll see."

Chapter 5

The following week commenced relatively uneventfully. Lara spent a few hours at the local Legal Aid office where she performed some basic grunt work from time to time. She went to classes and kept up with her reading.

Marcus came and sat with her and her friends in contracts on Tuesday, but she wouldn't exactly call it the highlight of her week. Things between them had definitely changed, for reasons Lara couldn't begin to fathom. He barely acknowledged her in fact, other than to make a cursory enquiry about her weekend, his voice strangely flat.

"Not bad. Yours?" she'd responded to his unsmiling face.

"Yeah, great, thanks," was all he'd given her, before turning away to engage Pete in conversation, a much more affable expression on his face. His earlier friendliness toward her had gone, and although he remained polite, she could only describe his manner as disinterested.

In the afternoon's criminal law class, he'd ignored her completely, sitting with Sally and Kristen and responding openly to their animated flirting, to their obvious delight. Go your hardest, you flake, she thought, trying to disregard the knot in her stomach.

During Thursday's criminal law class though, things deteriorated further. The topic was sentencing, and the recent federal legislation that had finally abolished the death penalty in every state and territory, as well as prohibiting it from ever being re-introduced. A group discussion got underway about the various international jurisdictions that condoned capital punishment, and the views of the Australian judiciary on the matter. Although it was inevitably a heated issue, it was to Lara's surprise that Marcus decided to weigh heavily into the debate from his place across the room.

"Well, I strongly disagree, with both you and the legislature," she heard him arguing with a classmate's viewpoint, his voice strong and clear. "In my view, there *is* a place for such sentences in this country right now, and there always will be! The criminals committing the most heinous of crimes—mass murderers for example—simply don't deserve misplaced sympathies and continued incarceration on the public's dollar. Entire families are out there being destroyed by these cold-blooded predators. And, all the while, the bleeding hearts are preventing us from using a powerful weapon in the war of deterrence against these monsters, a fact that has been statistically proven in numerous recent studies."

"What on earth are you talking about?" Lara heard her own involuntary and incredulous reply. "How can someone so educated be so archaic in their thinking? There's a reason why nobody has been executed in this country since 1967; it goes against all notions of human decency, not to mention our moral and ethical obligations under the Universal Declaration of Human Rights…"

"Which is *not* legally binding," Marcus interrupted. "Unlike the International Convention on Civil and Political Rights, which specifically permits the implementation of capital punishment…"

"*Plus*, the statistical studies you're talking about in relation to deterrence have had their methodologies questioned, while recent *psychological* studies have shown that most murders are impulsive acts, with the killers giving no thought to the consequences," Lara continued as if she hadn't been interrupted.

"Twenty-three percent of Australians have been shown to agree with me on this," Marcus retorted sharply, glowering.

"Yeah? Well, thank God the rest of us out here have the humanity and compassion to protect society from such a dangerous, backwards stance," she said before stopping her rant breathlessly. The stillness around her registered, and she was suddenly aware of how severe and passionate she had sounded. It was only then that she noticed how rigid Marcus's body had become, and how hard he was glaring at her, his blue eyes flashing with anger. When he opened his mouth a fraction, she flinched in anticipation of the verbal assault to come, until the tutor saved the moment.

"All right, enough for now! Thanks for your views, as many and varied as ever. Hopefully we've all learnt something and been given food for thought. That's what we're here for, after all. Take that passion home with you and use it to read up and bring me some A-grade papers on the topic of sentencing. Class dismissed."

Lara sat immobile as the chairs moved and scraped around her. Marcus briefly did the same, staring malevolently at her for an endless minute before deliberately turning and marching out of the room. Lara took a deep, shaky breath. What on earth had possessed her to speak so explosively to the one person she'd had any sort of interest in since she'd started uni? There was no doubt that she felt strongly about capital punishment, and was surprised to hear such an outdated opinion coming from him, but that didn't explain her fiery response. She could only think it was the tension that had been building between them that had caused her to fly off the handle in public.

Personal issues aside though, it was also frowned upon to denigrate someone's viewpoint so completely in such a conservative university course. She was mortified at her behavior. He must hate her now, if he hadn't already.

*

Later that day, after a contracts lecture during which Marcus had sat once again with the other girls and their friends, Lara joined Kate and Pete in the cafeteria.

"What on earth have you been up to?" asked Kate incredulously while Pete was ordering at the counter. "I heard about your little outburst in crim. It's not like you to talk up much in class, let alone to be so opinionated! And giving a rocket to the hottest guy in class…what were you thinking?"

Lara groaned and put her head in her hands, embarrassed to hear that their flare-up had become public knowledge. Kate sighed, and patted her on the shoulder.

"There, there…it'll all blow over. And I must admit, it sounds like he's got some weird opinions. Just don't let Pete hear about Marcus's fascist side. It'll tarnish his hero status in Pete's eyes!" Then, looking over Lara's shoulder, she continued in a muted but excited tone of voice.

"Speaking of James Dean, here comes our man…now's your chance to make amends."

Sure enough, Marcus came sauntering across the cafeteria in his faded jeans, bomber jacket, and scarf, his bag slung over his shoulder and his hair tousled from the wind outside. He did indeed look every bit the movie star. Lara felt her heart speed up involuntarily, especially when he pulled up a chair and sat down next to her. Once again, she could smell his maleness, and it was breathtaking.

"Hi there, Marcus!" said Kate in a sunny voice as she rose strategically from the table. "I'll get Pete to order one more coffee. Be right back."

And suddenly, it was just the two of them, sitting in silence. He wouldn't even look in her direction.

"Marcus, I'm…I don't know what to say about what happened earlier…" Lara stuttered in yet another attempted apology.

"Just forget it," he cut her off sharply. "Each to their own." He flashed her a dismissive glance before looking away again.

"Please!" She grabbed one of his hands impulsively, and noticed his eyes widen in a startled response as he looked back at her. "I was inexcusably rude to you again, and in public this time! I *completely* disagree with every word you said in class, but I'm not usually so hostile or unprofessional in the face of opposing viewpoints…I'm so, so sorry. My reactions to you just seem to be so extreme…"

Marcus simply stared at her a minute, his expression frozen on his face. Then she watched as he closed his eyes, raised his head, and took a deep breath, before exhaling slowly and looking back at her with a conflicted expression.

"Don't sweat it, sunshine," he said quietly. "As I say, each to their own, *on* their own," he added, extricating his hand from the grip that she'd unconsciously maintained, before turning his back to her and greeting Pete as he returned to the table.

Lara sat in silence, isolated in her embarrassment. Marcus couldn't have been clearer; apology *not* accepted. Well, she reasoned, she'd given it her best shot, but he clearly didn't want to be friends of any sort anymore. It was time to face that fact, and to simply push through the awkwardness and move on. Their already fragile connection was now severed completely, and she was responsible. She could kick herself for it over and over again, but it wouldn't achieve anything.

I'm an adult, and I'm perfectly capable of sharing friends with a hostile acquaintance, she thought. She squared her shoulders, held her head high, and joined in the group's conversation as though nothing had happened, pretending not to notice that Marcus no longer addressed her directly at all. And pretending that it didn't hurt.

*

The week after that was a lonely one. In Tuesday's and Thursday's criminal law tutorials, Marcus entered at the last minute, glanced almost imperceptibly around the room, and seemed to place himself as far from her as possible. In the bigger lectures, he either sat with Sally and Kristen, or came over to Lara and her friends but barely acknowledged her existence, while remaining as friendly as always with the others.

During her only visit to the cafeteria for the week, Lara had little to contribute to the usual social dialogue in her distracted state. Marcus seemed relaxed and calm there as he quizzed Pete in-depth about his musical tastes. But when he inadvertently reached for the sugar bowl at the same moment as Lara, his hand jerked away from the contact as if he'd been burnt, and she wondered if he might actually be more physically aware of her than he was letting on.

The final insult came late on Thursday afternoon. Lara had chosen to do some research in the library, because it was a typically quiet time of the week there, and relatively easy to access the highly sought-after computers. Out of the corner of her eye, she saw an imposing figure enter through the swinging doors and approach the only search terminal that remained free, right next to hers. She glanced sideways, only to realize with dismay that it was Marcus standing at the next desk, unraveling his scarf and taking off his jacket, obviously preparing to do some work. At that moment, he too looked up and recognized her with a start. It was evident from his obvious discomfort that he hadn't seen her until that moment, and wouldn't otherwise have chosen to be in such close proximity.

"Hi, Marcus," she said quietly, trying to restore some normality to the situation.

"Hey there," he responded, before returning his attention to some papers in his bag and mumbling something about having brought the wrong material with him. With that flimsy excuse, he picked up his things and walked straight back out of the library without saying another word.

Lara was offended and shaken by such an obvious rebuff, and for a minute, she was unsure what to do. Then she jumped up and marched out of the door with determination, leaving her belongings where they were. This sorry state of affairs had to be sorted out, and she was prepared to swallow her pride just long enough to have one more shot at reconciliation.

As she exited into the brisk air outside, she looked around to see which way Marcus had gone. At last, she saw him in the distance, striding toward a side exit of the campus. She ran after him, calling his name, but even as she closed on him, he continued ignoring her and kept walking away at the same furious pace.

"Hey!" she said loudly, reaching out and grabbing his arm when she'd finally caught up with him. He turned and glared at her in frustration.

"What do you *want*?"

"I just want to talk to you for a minute, like a civil human being!" she exclaimed. His eyes narrowed in response, and he pulled his sleeve abruptly out of her grasp.

"Now who's being the rude one?" she challenged him. He looked at her for a few moments in exasperation.

"Fair enough," he said through gritted teeth. "But the clock's ticking. Let's make it quick…I've got things to do." He certainly wasn't going to make this easy. Lara took a deep breath.

"Okay. Here it is. I *get* that we got off to a rocky start, despite one promising conversation out on the lawn, and I *get* that *you* don't seem to like *me* very much at all these days. I'm not sure exactly why you started feeling that way, but given what happened in crim last week, you're obviously now entitled to your opinion. But, having said that, this total cold shoulder approach of yours isn't very mature, or very fair. If your plan is to make me feel like complete crap, then well done, you've already well and truly succeeded. But if you keep it up, all you're going to do is make Pete and Kate feel really uncomfortable, and it's got nothing to do with them.

"So I'm officially waving the white flag and pleading for a truce. As distasteful as it might be to you, can't we give even a lukewarm friendship one more try, for everyone else's sake? There'll be no more verbal attacks from me, inside class or out, I swear."

Marcus stood still and regarded her with a frown, his lips pressed together tightly with tension. Finally, he reached up and rubbed his hands across his face a couple of times as if wiping it clean, before giving an audible groan.

"God, help me…" He sighed in exasperation. "Could this be any more dramatic?" She just looked at him, bemused, until he finally continued.

"All right, fine, you win! *Friends* it is, Lara. Mates. Pals." He shook his head mockingly as he spoke the words, but his sardonic expression slowly fell away as their eye contact held, until he was looking at her seriously, unsmiling.

With that change, Lara simply stared back at him, and for an endless moment, time stood still. Everything else disappeared as she withstood his appraisal and drank in his incredible beauty. Eventually, though, the rest of the world came flooding back when a chatting couple walked past them, and Lara was jolted out of her trance-like state.

"Well, all right then," she murmured. "We have a deal. Thank you."

"I've got to go." He broke their mutual absorption abruptly, taking a couple of backward steps away from her, but not breaking their gaze as he moved toward the gate. Raising a hand in her own wordless goodbye, Lara too moved backwards toward the library. They continued in this fashion, the distance between them increasing, but still facing each other, until Marcus finally whirled around and walked quickly away.

"Well, what am I supposed to make of that?" Lara murmured out loud. This guy blew so hot and cold that she couldn't keep up, but at least they seemed to have moved on from the last fortnight's "hostile" status. To what, she wasn't exactly sure.

Her confusion back with a vengeance, but proud that her determination had paid off, she sighed and continued on her way.

Chapter 6

All the talk on campus the following week was about the law ball, which was being held that Friday night. It was a big annual event on the university's social calendar. Black tie dress code, three course meals, bottomless drinks, live band—the works.

Lara had avoided it like the plague last year, not being a fan of loud, drunken crowds. But Kate wasn't letting her escape so easily this year. She'd jogged up to join Lara as they walked to their torts class, telling her that she'd already purchased both of their tickets. When Lara had started protesting that she already had plans to see her grandmother that weekend, Kate had cut her off at the pass.

"So hop on the first train to Geelong on Saturday morning, you social leper. There's no way you're leaving me to go alone!"

"You won't be alone," reminded Lara. "Pete will be there."

"Oh, please," replied Kate, rolling her eyes. "He'll be smashed before the entrée, you know that! And then off chatting up first years with his 'rock star' routine. Pleeeease, Lara. We've worked so hard already this semester, and this is a great chance to let our hair down for once."

"But I don't even have a formal dress," Lara continued to protest. "And I don't have the time or money to go and find one."

"I've got something you'll fit into," Kate pleaded. "Come on, girl, give it a go! You never know, Mr. Fabulous might be going…"

"I am," Pete confirmed with a wry grin, joining them as they entered the stream of students filing into the lecture theatre. "Oh, you mean Marcus? He's not; I've already asked. He's doing the he-man thing this week—gone bush. But there's no way you're getting out of it, Lara. You haven't lived until you've seen Pete Kingston bust a move on the dance floor, girl!"

Kate commented dryly that she was sure wild horses wouldn't keep any girl away, with that enticing image in mind. Laughing, Lara reluctantly agreed to go along, but couldn't help feeling oddly deflated after the absentee update.

*

Lara made her way to the city's glamorous Exhibition Buildings that Friday night wearing an old red evening dress of Kate's. It was a size too big for her, but Daniel had helped to make it look acceptable, belting it in with a black sash and selecting black accessories and makeup to offset the bright coloring. She'd caught her hair up in a simple French roll, having left herself short of time to make any greater effort.

"It's not perfect by any stretch of the imagination, but you'll do," Daniel had announced after appraising the finished product thoughtfully in her living room earlier in the evening, when he'd shared a glass of sparkling wine with her to help calm the ragged nerves.

"Gee, thanks for the vote of confidence, Daniel. Your admiration is simply overwhelming."

"I can only do my best with the materials provided, girlfriend," he'd responded with an exaggerated sigh. "I'm not a miracle worker. Now, go and have some fun, for God's sake! I want some good stories out of this, so go and do me proud."

The party was already in full swing by the time Lara entered the stately venue. Current and past students, as well as their many and varied friends, judging by the size of the crowd, were already seated at their allocated white-clothed tables, talking and laughing over the background music. After consulting a seating plan, she eventually found her way past the dance floor to the far side of the room. There, she found her friends playing a juvenile drinking game with others at their table, obviously instigated by Pete.

Grinning to herself as she joined them, she poured herself a glass of white wine and sank into a chair to watch the nonsense unfold.

Despite her usual avoidance of mass gatherings, Lara started to relax and enjoy herself, caught up in the festive and cheerful atmosphere. She surreptitiously observed her friends as they ate and drank, making legal jokes and conducting a mock trial over the relative merits of the chicken and steak dinners provided. She was proud and grateful to be among these intelligent, motivated people at this elegant affair. And just so glad she'd found the courage to come to Melbourne and enroll in this daunting university course, which had shaken up her simple world. What a fortunate life she led…the silver lining that had followed the heavy cloud of her father's death.

After main course, the lighting dimmed and the music started in earnest. Pete complained bitterly about the '80s hits that the DJ had chosen to start his set with, but it didn't stop him joining the droves of people piling onto the dance floor. Lara and Kate nearly laughed themselves sick watching him trying to chat up anyone in a dress, with very limited success, before deciding to join him under the colored lights and the disco ball, letting off some steam with a serious boogie. Even when Pete finally found a first-year student who was open to his advances, the girls kept dancing and singing along to song after song, stirred up by the energy of the night, until they finally fell into each other's arms and returned to the table, laughing and exhausted.

After a brief respite there, Kate moved away to chat with a judge's associate she knew, while a handsome third year guy they'd danced with for a while sidled immediately over and joined Lara for dessert. His name was Will Lancaster, and he was a blond pretty-boy. Lara knew that he was popular in female circles, and found him nice enough and very charming. They flirted innocently for a few minutes until the conversation got stuck on his carefully planned legal career, and she found her attention wandering.

It was only then that she looked across the room and, with a jolt, saw that Marcus had arrived. In a tuxedo that hung from his athletic frame like it was tailor-made, he was leaning against the wall near the entrance to the room, ankles crossed and beer in hand. He seemed to be looking her way, but she couldn't quite read his expression at that distance. Could he have been frowning?

Just then, cute, effervescent Sally from their criminal law class squealed and ran over to him, giving him a dramatic hug and kiss and dragging him back to her table across the room. Lara couldn't help admitting that the girl looked absolutely stunning, dressed to kill in a low-cut, golden satin and lace designer dress that set off her flaxen hair. She lost sight of the gorgeous pair as they moved past the dancing masses, which was probably just as well, as she was pretty sure her face would be reflecting her abruptly disheartened mood all too clearly. What was Marcus doing here? Had he come at Sally's invitation?

Feeling as sober as the proverbial judge all of a sudden, Lara excused herself during a pause in Will's dialogue, grabbed her evening bag, and disappeared into the sanctuary of the ladies' room. She shut herself in a private cubicle and sat on the toilet lid, taking a bit of time out from all the hype, and trying to make sense of her whirling thoughts. Just as she was preparing to emerge a couple of minutes later, she heard the bathroom door swing open again as some more girls entered to re-apply their makeup.

"I can't believe he actually came!" exclaimed an anonymous voice. "He looks even hotter in that suit than ever. Thank God I decided to buy this dress; it was worth every penny!"

"You are absolutely *in*, Sally! There's no way he'll knock you back looking like that. And you've got zero competition tonight… have you seen Lara? That dress looks like something my mother would wear! She's completely out of date."

Lara felt sick to her stomach hearing herself being discussed with such derision. All of the good feelings she'd had about the evening disappeared in an instant, and now she could only think about getting out of the place and returning to the safety of her apartment.

Mortified, she stayed where she was for a few minutes more until Sally and Kristen finally left the bathroom. Only then could she bring herself to emerge reluctantly from the cubicle. Once out, she took some deep breaths and splashed her pale face with water a couple of times, before drying herself off and re-applying her lipstick with a shaking hand. Finally, she stood up straight and tall and observed herself in the mirror. Then, as she so often did when someone or something had upset her, she conjured up her father's memory, in order to seek some of his endless wisdom and apply it to her problems.

"Don't let the bastards get you down," she whispered the well-remembered phrase to her reflection, which really wasn't all that bad. "Don't let the bastards get you down!" she said again, loud and proud, and laughed as an invisible cohort responded from the far cubicle: "You've got that right, sister."

She did. It was as simple as that.

Exiting the bathroom and returning to her table, Lara hung her small bag over the back of her chair and turned to the waiting Will.

"Would you like to dance?" she asked after taking a deep breath.

"I thought you'd never ask!" He grinned back. He really was extremely good looking, she thought. So what if he didn't set her world on fire? He was here, he was available, and he clearly didn't think she looked too shabby in the borrowed dress.

Holding out her hand with a smile, she received his gratefully and led him to the floor. The mood of the night had shifted by this later hour, and the music had slowed. Will pulled her toward him and they danced closely, sharing the occasional comment, but mainly just enjoying the music and the movement.

Lara smiled when she caught Kate winking at her from where

she sat back at their table with Pete, but her smile faded immediately when Will turned her a fraction and she saw Marcus and Sally dancing intimately together nearby. She quickly closed her eyes to block the view, determined to keep having a good time, and leant on Will's shoulder, eliciting an audible sigh of satisfaction from him. Nevertheless, by the end of the song, she was ready to move back to her friends for some comfort. She pulled her head up to excuse herself from Will's embrace just as a taller, darker figure put his hand on Will's arm.

"I'm afraid it's time I cut in, mate," Marcus said in a tone that brooked no argument.

But Will wasn't going to give in without a contest.

"I'm not so sure that's what the lady wants," he replied, keeping Lara in his grasp.

"I suppose you might be right," Marcus replied after a pause. "What *does* the lady want?" he turned and asked her directly, his look simmering. She took a few moments to respond.

"Thank you, Will, that was lovely," she said, turning to smile at him. "But it's time you freed up your dance card for some other lucky ladies, I think. I can see one girl who I'm pretty sure would love to take a turn with you." She nodded to where Sally now stood off to one side, obviously peeved at having been left alone. Will looked across at her before returning his gaze to Lara, completely ignoring Marcus as he did so.

"As you wish, I suppose," he shrugged good-naturedly. "It can't hurt to share ourselves around!" And with a genuine smile and a lingering peck on her cheek, he let Lara go and moved over to offer his services to the somewhat mollified Sally, leaving Lara to confront the next hurdle of the night.

Nervously, she forced herself to look up at Marcus's brooding face. He looked back at her silently for a moment, before taking one of her hands and pulling her gently toward him so he could wrap his other arm around her waist. Then they started moving slowly to the rhythm of the new song, allowing themselves to be absorbed into the crowd of couples dancing around them.

Slow dancing with Marcus was a different experience than dancing with Will. He was taller, for a start, so that Lara's head nestled naturally into his shoulder. In addition, he was a more confident and sophisticated dancer, who took complete control over the movements of her body, with his hand placed firmly at the small of her back. After a few moments of holding herself stiffly and shyly, Lara decided to let herself go, and gave in to the fluid, sensual motions as directed by him. She felt his body relax in response, so that they started moving as one under his expert guidance. It felt magical, and she closed her eyes and wished she could stay locked in his embrace forever.

Inevitably though, the song ended, and she made to move away from him regretfully, only to have him pull her wordlessly back against his body and tighten his hold for the next number, a slow, crooning Ella Fitzgerald song. Lara sighed contentedly, and allowed herself to get lost in the moment once again, until Marcus leaned down and breathed into her ear, sending a shiver up her spine.

"Mmmm, this is nice," he murmured, for only her to hear.

"Not to mention different…" she replied, half to herself.

"I suppose that's right," he said, and she could hear, rather than see, his ironic grin. "No one could ever accuse us of being boring!" Us.

"I wasn't expecting you to be here," she commented after a few moments.

"Last minute change of plans."

"Where have you been this week?"

"Away," he answered shortly, without further explanation. "Why? Miss me?" he teased, pulling his head back and smiling into her eyes. For the first time in weeks, he seemed completely relaxed and at ease, the barriers at bay.

"What? No…well, I guess we all wondered…" Lara stammered, as flustered as always, before taking a steadying breath and changing tack. "Well, in any event, I think Sally's pretty happy that you put in an appearance," she said, although Sally and Will were still dancing across from them, obviously having a pretty good time of their own. Marcus raised an eyebrow.

"Hmmm…noticed that, did you? Interesting. But just for the record, Lara, I couldn't care less what she or anyone else thinks," he replied. "And, between us, I'm not into blondes. Unlike yourself, apparently…"

"No, you're wrong…I'm not…so why did you come tonight then?" she said, deflecting his off-base comment in an effort to keep the conversation on track. "I wouldn't have thought this was really your scene."

"It's not."

"Then why are you here?" she asked again, but he didn't reply, turning instead so that his face was obscured from her line of sight. She lacked the focus or composure to quiz him further however, as Marcus spent the rest of the song pressed closely to her, brushing his cheek against her hairline and temple while humming softly to the music. Lara's heartbeat and breathing quickened. She was completely overcome by his sheer presence, her body reacting wildly to his every movement. Did he know what he was doing to her, she wondered? Although almost certain that he must, for once she didn't even care. She'd never felt such physical attraction in her life, and wasn't about to question something so powerful.

Utterly lost in sensation, Lara was still leaning into her perfect dance partner with her eyes closed when he spoke softly and brought her back to earth.

"I'm afraid the music's finished, sunshine," he said quietly, and she pulled back, embarrassed, realizing that the other dancers were already leaving the floor.

"Sorry," she mumbled, blushing. "Away with the fairies…"

"Right," he replied, his lips pressed together in amusement. "Thanks for the dance, Lara. It's been, well, interesting."

"Meaning?" she prompted him.

"Meaning, I'm glad I came," he clarified, giving her a small, private smile. "But it's time for me to move on, as I'm not technically supposed to be here. No ticket," he explained further at her questioning look. "So I'll leave you in the capable hands of your friends," he continued, leading her back toward the table where tea and coffee were now being served. "And away from the blonde bloke."

Marcus greeted Pete and Kate warmly and then made to leave, but Lara grabbed his arm to get his attention one last time.

"Marcus, wait!" she said quietly, and he stopped. "I just want you to know that I'm really glad we're friends again. Everything feels so much better now."

"It does feel good, doesn't it, being…friends," he agreed, but she couldn't help noticing that his smile wasn't quite reflected in his eyes. He took her hand off his arm and let it go with a tiny squeeze. "Until next time, then," he finished, before walking away. Lara's eyes didn't leave his departing figure until he'd exited the room.

"Having a good night?" Kate asked her with a nudge and a knowing smile.

Lara looked back at her, smiling self-consciously. "Well, first I was, then I wasn't, and now I am again. It's been a bit of a roller coaster. But, all in all, a real rush!"

"Good on you, sweetie! I'm so glad you came," laughed Kate, giving her a spontaneous hug.

"So am I, Kate. So am I."

Chapter 7

A week later, and Lara's relationship with Marcus had shifted yet again. The brief flirtation of the law ball had disappeared, and he didn't single her out in any particular way, but he now treated Lara exactly as he treated everyone else. And although she would have liked to have some time alone with him, she was mostly just glad that he was back to his former friendly, gentlemanly self.

Her thoughts were well and truly elsewhere however when Friday dawned, grey and drizzling. Difficult weather, for a difficult day. Lara lay in bed after a restless night that had been plagued by bad dreams. She stared at the ceiling with a heavy heart. It was two years to the day since she'd sat by her father's hospital bed and watched him take his final gasping breath—the worst day of her life. She still missed him all the time, but anniversaries like this were the hardest. As an only child whose mother had died when she was a baby, Lara and her dad had been as thick as thieves. He was the greatest man she'd ever known.

His health problems had been brought about by a horrific fishing boat accident when a gas bottle had exploded, giving him a chest full of shrapnel and third degree burns to his arms, chest, and neck. There'd been numerous operations, and Lara had undertaken more than her fair share of around-the-clock nursing duties over many months. But although he'd obviously been in severe pain, her father had remained his uncomplaining, tough self while cooped up in their beachside home. There was only one thing that had gotten the better of him toward the end—the despair and anger he'd directed toward the company that had manufactured the faulty bottle, which had resisted his claim for compensation. He and Lara had engaged a local solicitor to fight for their cause, but she was no match for the opposing team, who'd relied on dubious fine print and unwarranted delay tactics to ensure the matter went nowhere as Lara's father's health deteriorated and their bills mounted.

Lara had come to hate the faceless legal army for the additional pain they'd caused during those black days, and she'd promised her father that one day she'd be in a position to help protect others from such dismissive and condescending treatment. And so, after his funeral and the inevitable period of despair and numbness had passed, she'd sold their beloved home, paid off their debts, and moved in with her grandmother at the far end of town, before turning her mind firmly to her future. After finalizing her business studies by correspondence, she'd applied for the law course in Melbourne, desperate to get away from all of the painful memories. And she hadn't looked back.

After lying in bed and brooding a while longer, Lara eventually started getting organized for the day. She wore simple cargo pants and sneakers, with a black t-shirt and a black woolen jumper to match her mood. For once, she was late to class, slipping into the back row alone, listening to the lecturer's droning voice without even getting her books out of her bag. By the middle of the class though, she realized that she was feeling too numb and detached to absorb a thing, and that it was useless to remain there like a zombie. So she disappeared out the back door unnoticed, walking aimlessly across campus and feeling bleak and alone. It started to drizzle again as she walked past the deserted oval and running track, but she didn't care. In fact, she welcomed the freezing drops that stung her cold skin and tangled her hair, reminding her that she was very much alive and part of her surroundings. Her body was wired with unspoken emotion, but she couldn't think what to do with herself.

All at once though, she made a snap decision, and ducked under the fence of the deserted sporting field. Dumping her bag on a seat under a shelter, she broke into a spontaneous jog around the track. She took it easy for the first lap, raising her face up to the elements and allowing her muscles to warm up. Then, enjoying the relief from tension and despondency, she ramped it up a level until she got into a steady rhythm, her mind emptying of all thoughts, aware only of her steady breathing and pounding footsteps. In this trance-like state, Lara ran on and on, well in excess of her usual, measured pace. As fit as ever from countless hours of paddling into powerful waves, she lost track of the number of laps she'd completed, determined to continue despite the constriction of her wet pants, her now-laboring breath, and the onset of muscle fatigue.

In the end, however, she literally ran herself into the ground. Coming to a halt back near her bag, she fell onto her knees before sinking to lie sideways on the sodden grass, gasping for mouthfuls of air. And then, finally, thankfully, uncontrollable sobs of physical and emotional release arrived. Grief took over her body and mind, and for a time she allowed it to swallow her up.

Eventually though, her breathing slowed and her crying subsided along with the rain, until she fell silent, depleted of every ounce of energy. Other than to roll over and look directly up into the sky, she couldn't move a muscle. *God, what a complete mess I'm in*, she thought distantly. *Thank goodness I'm alone.*

Then, out of the blue, someone cleared his throat.

Lara sat bolt upright at the closeness of the sound, nearly jumping out of her skin in fright. To her amazement, the unwelcome interloper was Marcus, standing not a meter from her in a hooded raincoat, a look of deep concern on his face.

"What on earth are you doing here?" she gasped. *No, no, no,* her mind was yelling. Why did he have to be here right now, when she was at her absolute lowest in every way?

"I, um, watched you leave class early. You looked so sad; I just wanted to see if you were okay. I was about to call out to you when you came in here and started running. So I waited. But, now…I know something must be going on, but you can't just lie out here in the cold, Lara. You need to get out of those wet clothes, for a start. Please, you've got to get up."

With his kind words, her horror at being caught in such a compromised state dissolved. The angry response she'd formed at his intrusion died on her lips and, instead, unexpected tears welled up again in the eyes she'd thought had nothing left to cry. All she could do was bury her head in her hands, her defenses destroyed.

"I don't want you to see me like this," she managed to get out through her fingers, her voice cracking with emotion. Marcus responded by crouching down and gently taking hold of her elbows.

"Please," he repeated softly. "You're obviously having a really bad day. Let me help you."

Lara gave in and allowed herself to be pulled easily up into his muscular embrace. For a minute, she simply stood leaning into him, breathing in his scent mixed with the smell of the rain. Exhaustion registered, together with a sense of relief at having let go of her fierce independence, just for a time.

"Could you take me home?" she mumbled into his chest.

"My thoughts exactly," he replied, drawing her carefully to his side and walking slowly toward the gate while supporting most of her weight, stopping only to bend and pick up her bag on the way out.

*

His car turned out to be an old white pick-up truck. He opened the passenger door and half lifted her in, before snapping her seatbelt into place. Around the other side, he jumped in and fired up the engine, joining the congested lunchtime traffic outside the campus. After giving him her address, Lara leaned back against the bench seat with closed eyes, enjoying the blast of the heater against her frozen skin. Before she knew it though, he'd pulled up at the front of her house and was helping her out of the car and along the side path to the staircase.

Upstairs, Marcus rifled through her bag for the keys, fitted the right one into the lock, and pushed open the door.

"So this is where you live, Lara Lees," he uttered quietly from the threshold, looking around the tiny room with open curiosity before leading her inside and onto a chair. He then set about making the place warm, turning on a couple of lamps in the gloomy light, cranking up the gas heater, and going into the bathroom to run a bath. She could even smell that he'd added her favorite vanilla-scented bath salts to the hot water.

Lara couldn't do a thing to help, as by that stage, her teeth were chattering with cold and her body had started to shake. Marcus came back over to her and stood her up before pulling her sodden jumper over her head, taking off her shoes and socks, and even unbuttoning her pants and helping to wrestle the wet cotton down and off her legs. Pushing her gently into the bathroom, he threw her wet clothes into the trough.

"Get the rest of your things off and get straight in there before you get pneumonia," he instructed, pointing to the bath. "I'll be right out here, reading the newspaper, so don't worry about me. Just take as long as you need."

When he'd shut the door and left her alone, she tugged off her resistant t-shirt and underwear and climbed into the steaming tub. At first the heat hurt her icy body, but once she'd adjusted to the temperature, it was sheer bliss. She lay back, closed her eyes, and allowed herself to drift into a semi-conscious, vacant state where she remained for quite a while. After a while though, sighing reluctantly, she sat up and washed herself, before eventually climbing out and toweling herself dry. Then, dressing in the only clothes at hand—the same flannelette pajamas and bed socks she'd been wearing earlier that day—she ran a brush through her hair and looked in the mirror, dismayed at the sight of her pale skin and red eyes. But, faced with no choice, she took a steadying breath and opened the door into the living room.

There, she found Marcus as promised, sitting back on her couch in his shirtsleeves, reading the sports section of the day's paper. She noticed that a steaming cup of tea was waiting for her on the coffee table, next to his half-finished one. A lump formed in her throat as she observed the homely scene, with this amazing man at its center.

"Nice PJs," he commented as he folded up the paper, making her blush. "I figured you'd take your tea the same as your coffee, white with one?" he continued, smiling with satisfaction when she nodded and took the cup in both hands, before sitting down next to him.

"Well, you certainly look a damn sight better than you did," he remarked appraisingly. "Merely exhausted, as opposed to on the verge of collapse. You really drove yourself hard back there. It might be an idea to take it a bit easier next time." She took a couple of careful sips of the tea before responding, enjoying the sensation of the warm liquid flooding down her throat.

"Don't worry, that's not my usual approach to exercise." Lara paused before continuing, unused to sharing her most personal thoughts and feelings with anyone. But Marcus merely waited patiently, and so, taking a deep breath, she pushed through her self-imposed privacy barrier.

"My dad died two years ago today. It was always just the two of us, but then he was gone, and I still really, really miss him. The physical exertion back there helped to dull the pain," she finished simply. Marcus just stared at her, frowning in concern, before nodding his head in silent understanding. A minute went by before he said anything, and even then he spoke hesitantly.

"I understand what you're going through, Lara. My father was a cop, and he was shot and killed by a drug dealer during a raid," he admitted slowly. "That was nearly eight years ago now, and some days the grief still seems unbearable," he added. "So I get exactly where you're coming from. And racing your demons in the rain is actually a pretty good way to blow off steam, in the circumstances. It's better for you than most of the alternatives." He smiled, despite the sadness on his face. Lara just looked at him for a minute, speechless.

"That's an unbelievably terrible story. I'm so sorry, Marcus," she finally said in a quiet voice. *And now at least I understand your views on tougher sentencing laws*, she added to herself.

"As I am for you," he replied gently. "It's hard, losing a loved one—really, really hard. But time marches on, and as we know, whatever doesn't kill us only makes us stronger. So here we both are, tough as two old boots!" he said with a small smile, lifting the heavy atmosphere. Her dad would definitely have approved of this guy's positive attitude to life and living.

"So, tell me about the rest of your family," Lara asked, sipping her tea and curling herself up on the couch. "I'd love to get out of my own head for a while."

And he did. He talked of his mother and his younger sister Zoe at home in Sydney, describing their resilience, humor, and goodness. Aware of her need for distraction, he shared personal stories about his upbringing that brought a smile to her face: jokes that had been played, obscure family traditions, his mother's terrible cooking, and his sister's paralyzing fear of birds. Eventually, though, as Lara's eyes were getting almost too heavy for her to keep open, he stopped.

"Time to get you in bed, I think," he said quietly. She tried to argue, wanting to sit and listen to his resonant voice forever. But her extreme stress-induced fatigue got the better of her, and when he stood and pulled her into his arms, she simply sighed and gave in. As he directed her toward the bed and drew the curtains, however, her sense of loss returned.

"Please don't go! Not yet…" she pleaded, grabbing his hand as he returned to her bedside. He hesitated for a few moments before leaning down over her with a smile and smoothing the anxious lines from her forehead.

"I've got some things that have to be done this afternoon, Lara," he said. "But I'll tell you what…I'll stay here until you're asleep, okay? Deal? And I'll see you tomorrow night at Pete's gig, remember?" She nodded her agreement gratefully and allowed her eyes to close.

"Thanks again. I owe you one," she mumbled sleepily.

"Don't worry, I plan to collect one day," she thought she heard him reply. She felt the mattress shift as he sat on the bed next to her, leaning back against a couple of pillows. The last things she registered before drifting off to sleep were a gentle stroking of her hair and the soft humming of a barely perceptible tune. It felt safe. It felt like heaven.

Chapter 8

The following night, rested and restored, Lara slipped into a closely fitted black dress she'd found in a nearby retro store, and accessorized with some sparkling stockings, heels, and colorful glass jewelry. Next, she applied some striking charcoal makeup and piled her hair up with clips, leaving just a few tendrils to fall around her face. As someone who didn't bother dressing up to go out very often, she liked to have some fun with it when she did. And so, with a final satisfied check in the mirror, she headed out the door and made her way to find Pete and the others at the appointed hotel.

She entered the venue a little later than organized, just as Burst was warming up on stage. It was loud, crowded, and hot. She scoured the room and spotted Kate at a bar table off to one side with friends of the other three band members, some of whom Lara recognized. She registered immediately that Marcus was standing with them and drinking a beer, wearing a dark V-neck knit and some fitted black pants that suited his slim, athletic body to perfection. Dressed up, he looked even more amazing than ever, and Lara felt a pang of apprehension about seeing him again after the weirdness of the previous day.

As she made her way through the crowd, Pete noticed her arrival and gave her a thumbs up sign and a grin, causing the others to turn her way. Waving a hand in greeting, Kate raised her eyebrows and nodded her approval of Lara's outfit. But more noticeable by far was Marcus's reaction. He looked positively stunned when he saw her changed appearance, and her confidence soared.

After giving her a kiss on the cheek and a surreptitious "You look hot!" Kate went to buy them all a fresh round of drinks, leaving Marcus and Lara on their own, forced to stand so close in the noisy crowd that they were almost touching.

"Feeling okay now?" Marcus asked after a long pause, breaking the private silence.

"Fine, thanks again," she replied, as they continued openly assessing each other.

"This is a different look for you, then," said Marcus, finally.

"Yeah, well, I'd have worn my striped pajamas, but there's a dress code," she retorted lamely.

"You did look pretty cute in those pajamas, but..." His expression suddenly tightened, and he leaned even closer in to her, so that she could feel the heat emanating from his body. "You do know you look totally stunning tonight, I take it?" His voice rasped roughly at her ear, his comment meant for her alone. The hairs on the back of her neck rose and her heart raced.

"So do you, as always," she managed to reply, and they stared searchingly at each other as he straightened up again. Then, to Lara's surprise, Marcus reached up to secure a lock of her hair behind her ear, before allowing his fingertips to trail slowly back down the side of her face. Her heart pounding in her chest at this achingly intimate gesture, Lara felt a pull of attraction that was more powerful than anything she'd ever imagined. And this time, as they remained locked in each other's gaze, she had no doubt that the feeling was mutual.

But only a few moments after coming to this startling realization, she came crashing back down to earth as Marcus's face collapsed into a grimace and she heard his next words, uttered instinctively and in obvious frustration.

"What the hell am I doing? I'm so sorry..."

To her disappointment, Lara was given no opportunity to respond to his outburst, as an oblivious Kate chose that moment to return from the bar and start chatting to Lara about work. Then, giving her a final conflicted look, Marcus turned and entered a conversation with the lead singer's latest girlfriend, before the band started its first set and they all stopped to enjoy the music.

Burst really was getting very good, Lara thought, despite her distracted state. The band played original numbers only, and consisted of the sexy lead singer Charlie, Pete on guitar and backup vocals, and two scruffy muso brothers, Ted and Tony Jackson, on keyboards and drums. Charlie had boundless energy and kept the crowd completely engaged as the band moved between gritty rock songs and slower, yearning ballads.

Marcus appeared to be totally absorbed by the music, his body moving in subtle time to its rhythm. And although he glanced across at her occasionally and gave her a half-smile, he spent most of the time between sets chatting to the various connections of the other band members who were milling around nearby, while Lara stayed with Kate. She also thought she saw him make prolonged eye contact with an attractive redheaded girl who had joined the group, apparently a new friend of the Jackson brothers.

Angered by the unexpected wave of jealousy that swelled inside her, Lara deliberately turned away from him and forced herself to focus back on the band. There was no way that she was going to give in to such negative, poisonous emotions—life was just too short to go down that path.

Not long after the final song had come to a close and she'd had a chance to congratulate Pete on his performance, she and Kate decided to say their goodbyes to the group and call it a night. Marcus watched them as they made their way across the room, and Lara thought she might have detected a trace of regret in his gaze as they left him alone to hang out with the band. But then he turned back to Pete and the others with another beer in his hand, and she couldn't be sure.

And so the yo-yo effect continues. She sighed to herself as she left the building. Hot and cold, ebb and flow. The signals she got from this guy were all over the place, and she had no idea how he really felt about her.

Maybe it was time to find out.

*

On Tuesday the following week, after an unproductive remainder of the weekend during which Lara had mulled over the confused feelings that were so new to her, she came into uni earlier than usual. She'd decided to enjoy a quick coffee at one of the benches in the near-empty courtyard adjacent to the student building, before popping into the library for half an hour before class to look up an obscure case reference she'd come across.

As she took a seat, though, she looked up and saw Marcus observing her from the building entrance, holding a steaming cup of his own. An involuntary smile flooded her face and she raised her hand in an automatic greeting. But, to her embarrassment, he didn't return her smile. Instead, he regarded her seriously for a few moments before taking a deep breath and walking slowly across the space toward her.

Although as handsome as ever, he looked tired and a little disheveled, his hair windswept and his face unshaven. In addition to the backpack he carried over one shoulder, he was also holding a motorbike helmet.

"Hi," he said quietly as he sank down lightly onto the bench across from her, his expression guarded.

"Hi yourself," Lara said back, uncertainly.

"Have a good weekend?" he asked.

"It had its moments," she replied cryptically. "How about yours?"

"About the same."

"What's with the helmet?" she asked.

"It comes with a beaten up old Ducati I bought a while back. I've been riding it up north, and only just got back this morning. I guess I look pretty messy, huh?" He smiled sheepishly.

"You look just fine," she replied a little sarcastically, figuring he must know he looked more than fine, all the time. "Why haven't you mentioned the bike before?" Pete was going to go into raptures at the supreme coolness of this character. He really was James Dean reincarnated.

"I don't ride very often these days. A guy I know had a really bad bike accident a year ago, and I guess it hit home just how dangerous they can be. So I take it easy on the roads, but it's still a great way to blow off steam when I need to."

"And you needed to this weekend? Or are you just addicted to extreme sports?"

"Sort of both." Marcus couldn't help but smile. "I need a regular adrenaline rush to feel…balanced…living in the city. But I've also been doing a bit of soul searching, I suppose."

"Sounds intense."

"It has been." He looked into her eyes.

"So, did you find the answers you were looking for?"

"Kind of. There are no clear answers to some of my questions at the moment. But the one thing I've realized for certain is that it's time for me to back off."

"Right," said Lara, unsure about what he meant, but hearing warning bells all the same.

"Which leads me to the apology I need to make to you."

"You've really lost me now," Lara replied with a confused frown. "From where I'm sitting, you're the guy who saved me from myself when I literally ran into the ground a few days ago."

"That's not what I'm talking about." He shook his head.

"Then what?"

"I've been giving you certain—signals—lately, which have been way out of line. I know you know what I mean. You're a beautiful woman, so I'm sure you're used to male admiration. But I've been acting without thinking, and I need to clear something up. Lara, I *like* being your friend, and I *like* being part of such a great group of people, and I don't want to mess with that. Please understand, it's nothing personal, but I'm not interested in dating you, or in anything more than friendship. And if I've led you to believe otherwise, I'm sorry."

Lara became very still as she absorbed his words. So there it was, the bucket of cold water over the pathetic daydreams that had been floating around in the back of her mind. She'd been completely kidding herself, thinking he might have had an interest in her that was more than skin deep! A guy like him… such obvious heartbreak material. She felt like a complete fool, and was furious with herself for allowing her hopes to be raised.

But, thankfully, along with the bitter sting of rejection, Lara's indignation surfaced. Marcus and his flakey, inconsistent attitude could go to hell! She was damned if she was going to let him or anyone else mess with her head in this way, or see how much he'd hurt her feelings. So, burying her self-pity for a time, she focused all of her efforts into playing the role of the easy-going woman of the world, instead of the simpering victim. And with that determination to maintain her dignity, she wrested control of the conversation, and returned his concerned expression with a seemingly nonchalant one.

"Oh, right, I see. Well, thanks for the heads-up. Message received loud and clear." She shrugged. "Friendship—green light. Romance—off-limits. Gotcha."

"Is that all right with you then? You're not angry or upset with me or anything?" He looked confused.

"Not at all!" Lara even managed a half-smile. "Things are what they are. I'm good either way."

"Oh. Okay. Great, then," he responded uncertainly, running his hands through his tousled hair while he registered the about-face of the conversation. Lara could almost have laughed out loud; she couldn't believe she had the great Marcus Black off-balance! Well, it was no more than he deserved.

"It's just that, well, I just thought…" He paused. "We seemed to have had some sort of connection at the ball, and then at the start of Pete's gig. I got the impression you might have been, you know, keen for…"

"Marcus, say no more, honestly! Let me clear a couple of things up for you." Lara leaned forward with a blasé smile and squeezed one of his hands in an Oscar-winning performance. "I've got my mind set on only one thing this year, and that's to excel in this course. I love hanging out with you guys in the meantime, and a romantic interlude here and there is always fun, but it's no more than a distraction." She shrugged again. "And sure, you're a great guy, and very good looking," she almost choked the words out, "but, to be frank, you're not my usual type anyway. As you say, it's nothing personal." Take that, heartbreaker.

"No, no, of course not," he replied quietly, after a pause. "I see. Well, I guess that's good news then." He pulled his hand away from hers. His expression was now veiled and unreadable; the slight frown could have been disappointment or just incredulity. He was undoubtedly used to calling all of the shots, all of the time. A world where a woman failed to fall at his feet probably made no sense to him at all.

"Great! So no harm done here," Lara said. "Let's just keep on keeping on; business as usual. Speaking of which, probably time for me to get a move on," she added brightly, looking at the time and giving a fake yawn and a stretch. "I'll see you in class though, no doubt."

"No doubt," he repeated, looking back at her, immobile.

"Well, bye for now," she finished, picking up her bag and walking away with a casual wave, before making her way to the very back of the law library.

And only there, safely hidden from her fellow students, did Lara allow her false brightness to fade. She put her head in her hands with a groan, leaning on the desk as she mentally replayed the conversation, forcing their relationship status to sink in fully. It was a real kick in the guts after their recent closeness—no doubt about that. But, to her relief, she also realized that it was bearable. After all, things between them hadn't progressed beyond mere flirtation, and she was a realist, not a fool. She was better off on her own. Less chance of being knocked for six that way.

Chapter 9

Over the next few weeks, a pattern of sorts developed, as Marcus was further absorbed into Lara's friendship group. If the others noticed that her attitude toward him had become more businesslike, they didn't mention it, and Marcus's own polite public behavior seemed unchanged. While Lara initially kept her distance from him after their heart-to-heart, it wasn't long before the two of them re-discovered a comfortable co-existence, and then a companionship.

They invariably sat together in lectures these days, including in criminal law, much to Sally's obvious disappointment and Lara's distraction. Thursday afternoon sessions in the cafeteria became a regular hangout. Marcus and Pete in particular really hit it off, and a couple of times they left together in the evenings to hang out at Pete's place and listen to new music that one of them had bought.

Marcus proved to be a good study partner too. Given her lack of reliance on summarized notes, Lara did the majority of her study alone each year. But at this point in the semester when the various essays were piling high, deadlines were looming, and tests were imminent, the sheer volume of material to be covered for each class necessitated a "divide and conquer" approach. In the past, she'd split the research tasks with Kate, as Pete was the first to admit that he was insufficiently reliable to be involved. But this semester, Marcus joined their study group as well. The threesome booked one of the soundproof meeting rooms in the library every Friday afternoon to distribute and discuss their respective research notes for the week, ensuring that they could fully cover the assessed topics in both contracts and torts.

The newest addition to their group turned out to be very thorough, and almost as bright as Kate, impressing them both with his ability to think on his feet and debate the legal points at hand. But, being blessed with an outstanding memory, Lara outdid the others when it came to being able to identify the subtle differences in the various judgments covered, and therefore to predict the likely future direction of the judges' decision-making. They all had their strengths.

"We should open up a boutique law firm," said Kate at the end of one particularly lengthy session, as she organized her notes. "No joke. You should meet some of the idiots I work for, and yet somehow they make a more than decent living. We've got all of the necessary skills between us, believe me. I reckon we'd make a killing!"

"Except that Marcus wants to be a prosecutor," Lara interjected. "Anyway, Kate, how would Pete fit into this mythical firm of ours, do you reckon? Organizing the annual Christmas party?"

"He could be useful in business development, I suppose," Kate replied with a grin. "He'd be able to bring in some of his dodgy nocturnal mates as clients. Some of them will undoubtedly need a good defense team at some stage."

"What do you mean?" asked Marcus, interested. "Does Pete know some crims?"

"Oops, look out! Pete's just been red-flagged. You might want to stay away from him from now on, Marcus. I mean, a friendship with such an unsavory type mightn't look so good on an up-and-coming prosecutor's resume…" Lara joked. Marcus merely threw a paperclip at her in reply, accidentally upending his bag of notes on the floor as he did so.

"Hey, enough of that slanderous talk." Kate laughed, bending down to help Marcus retrieve the lost load. "I just meant that Pete probably comes across the odd crook late at night in his pubs and clubs, wouldn't you think?"

"Probably." Marcus smiled, gathering up some of the scattered papers.

"Here you go," said Kate, handing him back a wad that included a neatly labeled manila folder. "'Operational Data.' Wow, what's this? Sounds intriguing! Is it—?"

But before she could finish, Marcus reached across and snatched the file roughly out of her hands at lightning speed, a black look on his face. The girls stared at him wordlessly, watching in puzzlement as he seemed to forcibly relax his body and regain a more normal facial expression.

"Sorry, Kate, I didn't mean to be rude. That's just some research I'm doing for a friend. I've given an undertaking that it'll remain completely confidential."

"Oh, I see," Kate replied uncertainly. "I didn't mean to pry."

"I know." Marcus smiled weakly, before stuffing the remaining notes into his bag and standing with a stretch. "Well, thanks again, ladies. Couldn't do this without you."

"Likewise," replied Kate, rising to join him. "A problem shared is a problem halved, or so they say. Let's just hope we can all hang in there and not collapse from exhaustion in the meantime though."

*

On the following Tuesday, after days of windy, showery weather, the sun actually came out to warm the earth. Lara broke away from the pack after contracts, bought some sushi for lunch, and found a spot on the expansive university lawn to enjoy an hour of much-needed time outside. She lay back on the grass and stared up at the sky, loving the touch of the light northerly breeze against her skin. An early reminder of the spring days to come, and the offshore wind that promised some superb surfing conditions. She sighed with pleasure at the mere thought. Just then, though, her dream state was interrupted.

"Knock, knock," a familiar voice said.

"Who's there?" She smiled without breaking her gaze away from the endless blue sky.

"A fellow fresh air freak," Marcus responded.

"Then come and join the fun," she offered and rolled lazily onto her side as he joined her, too happy with the day to feel unsettled. "Isn't this heavenly?"

"About time! I've been going crazy indoors. I can't wait for mid-semester break."

"Mmm, me neither. What're you going to do?"

"I'm joining a mate for a hike in the Otway Ranges for a few days. Other than that, just taking it easy. How about you?"

"I won't be far from you, at Anglesea, enjoying the surf and some time at home," she replied. "It's a fantastic time of year there. Good weather, no crowds."

"Tell me about home," he asked, lying opposite her and propping himself up on one elbow. So she did, cautiously at first, until she inevitably warmed up to her favorite subject. She described Gran and her house, the crosswords and game shows, her rambunctious Chief, the emptiness of the dunes, and the endlessly changing conditions on the back beach. Then she talked about surfing…the sheer exhilaration of riding down an unbroken wave, skimming silently across the surface of the water and enjoying everything that mother nature had to offer.

As she spoke, Lara realized that she was actually enjoying sharing such an important part of herself with Marcus. He was an interesting friend to have, if nothing else. She'd even come to agree that a relationship might've been an undesirable complication in her university life at this point…maybe he really *had* done her a favor by pulling back.

For his own part, Marcus seemed to like listening to her talk, watching her face light up as she spoke passionately about her great loves with an intense but unreadable expression.

"I'll have to head there sometime," he mused, as she finished painting her verbal picture of Anglesea. "The swells sound awesome! Although maybe a bit much for a hack surfer like myself. Sounds like you're a lot better on a board than I am."

"I'm all right." She shrugged. "No better or worse than anyone else who grew up on the coast. We've all got salt water in our blood. How often have you surfed?"

"I've given it a go a couple of times, but I'm certainly no expert. More of a kayaking guy, really."

"Well, you can always pop in and visit Gran and me if you have time while you're down that way," Lara offered without thinking. "I've got a spare board—you could test yourself out in the waves. I guarantee you'd love it." It was only when he looked at her questioningly that she realized he might have misinterpreted her offer.

"I mean, we have people drop by all the time. The others might even be coming down there these holidays," she added hastily. "Totally up to you, of course."

He continued to observe her silently for a few moments before responding carefully. "It all sounds very enticing, I must say. I'll keep it in mind. And while we're doling out invitations, any interest in coming to see Burst again this Saturday at the Tote? I'm going, and Kate's coming with her Matt."

"Umm, I'm not sure," Lara said, buying some time as she thought through the pros and cons of his offer. Although she'd managed to harden herself toward Marcus and his charms since their recent reality check, common sense still told her to keep some distance. She didn't want to allow him, or anyone else for that matter, the chance to get through her defenses ever again.

"Oh, come on!" he urged. "Couldn't you do with a break from all of this work? I know I could; I've even started dreaming about the damned cases we're studying. It's time to get a life back, even if it's only for one night! Let's all go together."

"Let me think about it," Lara replied, still unconvinced.

"Fair enough." Marcus sat up after looking at his watch. "Anyway, time's up, I'm afraid. Class is about to start," he added, standing and holding out his hand to pull her easily up to him. He held onto her hand a fraction longer than she'd expected, before giving it a brief squeeze and pulling away. Without warning or invitation, a frisson of remembered excitement fired through Lara's body at their physical contact.

Her cheeks flamed with emotion. Although she was careful to conceal her confusion while brushing herself down and collecting her belongings, there was no hiding her sudden realization from herself. As they walked toward the law buildings, she acknowledged with dismay that she was still infatuated with Marcus, despite weeks of sensible self-talk. Where was her pride, or her self-preservation? For his part, Marcus certainly didn't seem to be similarly affected, chatting about the pending tutorial as they walked.

Sighing to herself, Lara tried to ignore the pit in her stomach and accept the fact that guys' feelings were just less intense and enduring than girls'. Marcus had made it clear how he felt about her, and if she knew what was best for her, she should continue to respond in kind.

Chapter 10

By that Saturday night however, Lara had decided that she would put the books aside for a while and go out with the others—and she'd managed to convince Daniel to join them.

This time, she wore a sparkling beaded silk top that draped across her collarbone and fell in shimmering, pale golden waves to where it was gathered by a wide belt at her hips, before hanging over some tight leggings tucked into heeled boots. She put her hair back in a severe high ponytail, but her makeup was softer than the last time she'd been out, her eyelids cream and gold with a more neutral lipstick. Just as she was applying the finishing touches to her face and spraying on some perfume, there was a knock at the door. She smiled and opened it wide, only to be greeted by a lewd wolf-whistle.

"Wow! Who're you, and what've you done with my frumpy housemate?" asked Daniel, nodding in approval.

"You don't look so bad yourself, handsome," she retorted, giving him a kiss on the cheek. In fact, he looked fabulous in charcoal pants and a clinging black top under his standard leather jacket. And she noticed that the usual bling had been replaced by just a tiny amount of hair product, a smudge of black eyeliner, and some classy aftershave.

"How are you feeling?" she asked.

"Pretty cool." He smiled. He'd finally plucked up the courage to ask the captivating businessman from his café to join them this evening, and the man (named Dan, coincidentally) had accepted without hesitation. Daniel was beside himself with anticipation, and Lara couldn't wait to meet the guy she'd heard so much about.

"How about you, Lara? Looking forward to some dirty dancing with *your* beau?" Daniel joked.

"Hardly likely." Lara rolled her eyes. "Don't forget that I'm *persona non grata* as far as he's concerned, at least in the love-life department. I'll be lucky to get so much as a peck on the cheek out of him! Anyway, with someone like him, there's just too much background noise for a girl with any sense to be romantically interested."

"He sounds totally weird." Daniel repeated the opinion he'd held for weeks now, after his initial urgings. "What's not to like about *you*? Wait until I give him a piece of my mind!"

"You'd better not, or I'll tell Dan the Man all about your former exploits. He might not be quite so keen on you if he finds out what sort of a tramp he's hooking up with! I mean it, Daniel, I've managed to forge a comfortable existence with Marcus, and if you mess with all my hard work I'll never forgive you."

"Relax, sweetheart! Tonight's not all about you, you know. Some of us will have more on our plates than trying to stoke up your pathetic love life."

The pair of them continued their easy joking and teasing as they made their way toward the iconic live music venue in the adjacent suburb, where the band was already tuning up. Dan didn't seem to have arrived yet, so Daniel went to the bar to buy them both a drink, while Lara started to make her way to the side of the room where the band's friends had congregated. Lara saw Kate and Matt, who were obviously loving being out together, their arms wrapped firmly around one other as they chatted.

Then she saw Marcus, who turned at the same moment and caught sight of her. For a few moments, he simply took in her appearance. Then his piercing blue eyes looked up until they were gazing directly into her own. And they told her a story. A story that didn't match his rhetoric.

For the first time in a while, she was permitted past the well-crafted surface to witness the true yearning and conflict within. With only a look, he let her know that, despite what he'd said to her previously, he wanted her, and more importantly, that he cared. Lara's heart leapt in response to this stunning revelation as the rest of the world disappeared…she'd never felt so connected to another human being in her life. The carefully constructed caution of the last month or so went to the wind, and her instinctive feelings for this man came flooding back to the surface. Taking a deep breath, she took the final few steps toward him slowly and deliberately, until they stood only centimeters apart, staring at each other for a long, long minute.

"So," he said finally, after clearing his throat.

"So," she agreed.

"Here we are again. And yet…"

"Yes."

"You look absolutely breathtaking, Lara."

"Thank you."

"We really have to talk."

"We will. Another time." Lara was about to continue when he suddenly straightened up, the intensity of his expression replaced by a neutral smile, as Kate and Matt came to greet her.

"Lara! You did come after all—excellent! And I see that Marcus has already found you? Hmm." But Kate's prying was quickly waylaid by her more polite boyfriend's elbow, as he greeted Lara with a hug and some welcome small talk. Then, just as Kate had reclaimed Matt's attention and Marcus had given Lara another private smile, Daniel arrived.

"Hi there, guys. Here you go, babe!" he announced in his extraverted fashion, handing Lara her drink and putting his free arm around her. "I got your favorite, a champagne cocktail. Sweets for the sweet."

But Lara wasn't listening to him. She was watching in disbelief, as Marcus's entire being transformed before her very eyes. His smile fell away in an instant and his eyes turned to flint. He seemed to be glaring at Daniel with a look bordering on hatred. What on earth was going on? Did they know each other? Or could she have totally misread Marcus, and set her sights on a narrow-minded homophobe? Her mind reeled, distraught with the possibilities.

"And you are…?" Marcus almost spat at Daniel, who was returning his hostile look with one of interest.

"I'm Daniel, my friend. Lara's neighbor and greatest fan. And I think I can guess who you might be!" While Marcus continued to glare explosively at Daniel in some kind of one-sided male standoff, Daniel became more and more visibly amused. The situation was getting absurd, Lara thought, still at a loss as to what was going on; the moods of the two men were completely mismatched. Eventually, Daniel turned to address Lara, ignoring Marcus's existence completely.

"Okay. So here's my take on your situation, honey." Lara thought she saw Marcus's body tense even further at the endearment. "I can see why you've been so taken with your friend here. He's bloody divine…well done! And I don't think I've ever seen such a manly display in my life—beautiful stuff! More importantly, though, you don't have to worry about the crap he's been feeding you about only wanting to be friends. He wants much, much more than that, trust me. So much so that my presence here with you is eating him alive! Don't you see? His gaydar isn't switched on—he thinks I'm a threat!"

Daniel started to chuckle, and his laughter became even more raucous as he watched the ensuing wave of emotions sweep across Marcus's face with his words. First confusion and uncertainty, then dawning realization and, finally, embarrassment. Daniel was having a field day!

"Oh, this is gold! Wait until I tell the other guys! Anyway, I'll leave you two to sort yourselves out without me now, if you can. My own gorgeous date has just turned up, and he needs some attention. Ta-da!" And with that, Daniel gave Lara a kiss on the cheek and flounced across the room toward a handsome blond man, whose eyes lit up when he saw Daniel approaching.

When he'd left, Marcus ran a hand across his chin and stood for a few moments with his head bowed and his teeth clenched. Finally, he looked back up at Lara, regret in his eyes, and took a deep breath.

"Right. Well, this is awkward, on a number of levels. You must think I'm a world-class idiot," he said. "I'm really sorry about that—I didn't mean any offence. I think your friend was right; my territorial male instincts seem to have taken over in the heat of the moment. Just call me Neanderthal Man. How pathetically primeval we men are in the presence of a beautiful woman. Forgive me?"

"Of course." Lara laughed in response, hiding the secret joy she felt at his possessiveness. "Although I'm never going to hear the end of this from Daniel. He likes you, though, I can tell, despite the fact that the feeling obviously wasn't mutual a couple of minutes ago! Maybe just buy him and his friend a drink, and I'm sure there'll be no hard feelings."

"Good thinking. I will. It's the least I can do. And Lara, about those other things Daniel was saying, I don't think…" He stopped and looked away uncomfortably, clearly unsure how to proceed. Lara smiled, amused that this unbelievably attractive man was actually at a loss for words. But she decided to let him off the hook.

"Come on, let's leave that for now. I think it's time to join the others and give Pete a show of support, don't you? There'll be plenty of time for us to talk later."

Marcus smiled back in relief and joined her near the front of the room with the others while the band started their first set. Daniel and Dan eventually joined them, and Marcus immediately embraced Daniel in a giant hug that lifted him off the ground. The pair rehashed their misunderstanding between bouts of laughter while Lara chatted with Dan, whom she found to be absolutely delightful. Then they all got into the music, singing along and dancing during the better-known numbers, and cheering loudly at the end of each one. Lara was having the best night!

At one stage, she noticed the pretty redhead from the previous gig watching Marcus, but she didn't care a bit. *Lara* was the one he was smiling at and dancing with tonight, the one he was letting inside. It was her night, and she glowed with happiness.

*

Later on, after Kate and Matt had left, Daniel signaled to Lara that he and Dan were heading home as well, and she decided to join them. To her surprise and disappointment, Marcus announced that he was going to stay out with Pete and the other guys, and head to a dance club in the city. Her feelings were immediately appeased however when he pulled her gently aside and asked whether they could get together the following day. When she'd smiled her assent, he gave her a long, intimate hug goodbye, and seemed as reluctant as she was to break the contact and move away.

After the rest of their goodbyes, Lara, Daniel, and Dan headed out onto the near-empty street. The threesome started walking toward the suburb of Carlton, arm-in-arm and singing one of the band's songs, badly. They were only about a hundred meters down the road however, busy laughing and joking together, when Lara realized that they weren't alone. She turned swiftly to find two men from the pub right behind them, already uncomfortably close. With dismay, she registered three things simultaneously: they were very big, very drunk, and their faces were ugly with contempt. The hairs on the back of her neck rose instinctively.

"Well, look what we have here, Mac!" one of them spat. "A couple of filthy fags and a fag-hag." The boys stopped and turned. Daniel moved protectively in front of his mate.

"Wandering around our streets, as happy as you please," scoffed the second man.

"Hey, take it easy, fellas! We're just going about our business; we're not trying to get in anyone's way," said Dan, his hands held palm outwards in front of him in a conciliatory gesture.

"Well I've got news for you, you pack of freaks, you *are* in my way! You're not welcome in these parts… Get the hell out of here and don't come back!" the second man continued, almost snarling. Lara made to back away from them, trying to pull Daniel's arm along with her. But she should have known it wasn't in his makeup to retreat from a verbal assault on his very nature, in his part of town.

"It's our neighborhood too, you rednecks! Do everyone a favor and bugger off to whatever stinking halfway house you came from."

That was all the provocation the two men needed. One of them grinned nastily; he'd obviously been spoiling for a fight and saw what lay ahead. To Lara's horror, the other undid his belt buckle and slipped off his thick leather belt in a single, effortless motion, holding it up to make sure his evil intentions were clear. Lara's blood went cold.

"No, please, we don't want any trouble…" she pleaded, stumbling back a couple of steps. But her words fell on deaf ears; the attack had already begun. The men stepped forward in unison and each selected a male victim. Daniel made a valiant attempt at fighting back, trying to dodge punches and lay a couple of blows himself, but he didn't stand a chance against his attacker's superior strength and technique. He was thrown to the ground almost immediately, and, to Lara's disgust, his mugger started laying the boot in. He kicked repeatedly with brute force, the sounds of his primal grunts muffled by the more sickening cries and gasps of her distraught friend.

Worse still was the beating Dan was enduring. His assailant threw him almost immediately to the ground and started whipping him with the belt buckle. While Dan tried to protect himself from the worst of the assault by curling into a ball and covering his head, Lara could see that his arms were bleeding. Prompted into action by the sight of the cuts, Lara yelled out and forced her shocked body to move. She grabbed the belt as the monster came in for his third strike and pulled hard, so that he became unbalanced and almost toppled to the ground. But he righted himself just in time and looked at her with loathing, before ramming his bulky body into her slight one. She flew backwards off her feet and landed on the pavement, knocking her head hard, dazed and hurt.

The events that followed were blurrier. Lara heard someone shouting for help, and then there was a lot of yelling and running footsteps, before the cavalry arrived. The sound of more punches and animal grunting, before a strong voice took control and issued orders. She rolled onto her side with a groan and opened her eyes, trying to focus on the scene.

There was Marcus, pushing down one of the aggressors, his knee lodged firmly in the small of the man's back while twisting one of his meaty arms behind him. Whatever he was doing was obviously effective, as the man was whimpering like a baby. Then she noticed Pete and Charlie sitting on the other bloke, grinding his head into the ground and talking trash while the Jackson brothers each rendered an arm immobile. A small crowd of night prowlers was also gathering, excited and animated.

Next, Lara saw Marcus hissing into his cell phone, before he closed it and looked across at her in alarm. "It's okay," he mouthed silently in the growing din, his eyes throwing her a lifeline amongst the confusion. She nodded once before finally allowing her eyes to close, her body slumping in shock and relief now that she knew they were safe.

Other images and sounds fought their way through her brain's fog. A car arriving. More shouting. A hand stroking her forehead and her hair, someone squeezing her hand. A familiar voice…

"Everything's all right, I'm right here." Sirens approaching, then a different voice… "Hey, mate, what have you stumbled into?" Hushed voices. A neck brace and a stretcher. A boost into an ambulance and being driven at speed. The handhold unbroken.

"Daniel?"

"He's fine. Just rest now."

"Those guys?"

"It's all okay, I already told you. Shhh."

Blessed sleep.

Chapter 11

Lara came to a short time later in a hospital. She was lying in a cubicle in a busy emergency department, with Pete sitting by her side. She had one hell of a headache, and when she reached to touch the back of her head, she felt an egg-shaped lump. She winced, before asking Pete for a glass of water. He called across to a nurse, who came and undertook a brief examination. She tested Lara's vital signs as well as her neck mobility, pain level, and memory. Then she left again, after confirming that all was normal.

"Thank God, Lara!" Pete exclaimed and sat back in his chair with obvious relief. "We were all concerned when we heard you'd lost consciousness for a minute there! How are you feeling?"

"Like I've had a huge night out. Where are we?"

"St. Vincent's. Daniel and his friend are here too, in different cubicles. And before you ask, they're fine, apart from a few impressive cuts and bruises. Daniel's got some stitches on his side, where that moron kept kicking him, and his mate has a couple on his neck. The doctors want to keep all three of you here for a couple of hours for observation, just to make sure you're not badly concussed."

"Where are those two animals?"

"They were carted off in a divvy van, don't worry." Pete grinned. "They'll be in lock-up by now, hopefully receiving a bit of their own medicine from some other drunken cowboys. Charges will be laid before morning. What a pair of losers…it's depressing to realize there are still bigots like them around. Poor Daniel and Dan. Life's tough enough without having to deal with that sort of crap."

"Well, I guess we're all still here to tell the tale," Lara said, smiling weakly. "Sorry it's been such a rotten end to your big night. But I really do appreciate you riding in the ambulance with me, and all of your support."

"Your appreciation on that front is undeserved I'm afraid," Pete said, an amused expression on his face.

"Why's that?" Lara asked.

"Because it wasn't me."

"What?"

"Marcus accompanied you here."

"Oh. Huh!"

"Your white knight…he's the real rock star tonight," Pete said. "You should have seen it, Lara! As soon as we walked out of the pub, Marcus saw what was going on, bolted over to you all, and started giving those freaks an absolute dust up. They didn't stand a chance! I've never seen anyone get control of a fight so easily. We all helped him out, keeping the two guys on the ground until the cops arrived, but only on Marcus's instructions. He knew exactly what to do, and was just as calm and cool as you like…" Pete shook his head in obvious admiration and wonder.

"Until he realized the state *you* were in, that is…" he continued. "As soon as he could get free he was at your side, and he wouldn't budge. I tried to get into the ambulance with you, but he just glared at me, and wouldn't let go of your hand. By that stage he looked completely stressed out, so I just let it go and hopped in with Daniel and Dan."

"So where is he now then?" Lara asked.

"Who knows? As soon as he heard from the docs that you'd be all right, he said he had to take care of a couple of things, but that he'd be back. That was about fifteen minutes ago. It's nearly one o'clock now."

"Oh God, Pete, is it? I've really cut into your night. Why don't you head off? There's still time for you to catch up with the others and continue the party. I'll probably just nap, if I have to stay, and Daniel and I can catch a cab home together. Go on, you've done your bit," she assured him. "Just check in on the others on your way out for me, okay?"

After some minor resistance, Pete agreed. He walked along the corridor for a minute before returning with a smile and some old magazines nabbed from the waiting room.

"I think your boys must be feeling better. They've already given a statement to the cops, and now Daniel's in his friend's cubicle at the end of the hall, holding his hand! The nurse doesn't look overly impressed that he's left his own bed, but he insists he's fine. Anyway, they said they'll come by and grab you when you're all released on parole. So I'll love you and leave you." He leaned down and gave her a peck on the cheek. "I'll call Kate on my way home, too. I rang her earlier, and she was all set to traipse down here to join your well-wishers. But I'll tell her that you'll just call us both tomorrow so we know you're okay."

"Sure thing. Thanks." Lara smiled back, and he left. Then she lay back with a sigh and let herself doze off again in the antiseptic, surreal environment. The next thing she knew, she was being shaken gently awake.

"Lara, it's me, Marcus. Sorry, but it's time to wake up now. The hospital is discharging you and your friends, and they need the bed." She opened her eyes groggily, taking a minute to remember where she was and what had happened. As she sat up though, the ache in her head was a helpful reminder. Marcus was standing right beside her, watching her with concern. Then, after making room for a harried nurse to do some final checks, he stepped back in and steadied her as she stood, swaying slightly until she got her land legs.

"Thanks," Lara said. She was so glad he was here with her.

"No problem," he replied. "What bad luck you all had running into that pair of thugs! How are you feeling now?"

"Not too bad. Just tired, mainly."

"No wonder; it's super late. Let's get you home."

It turned out that Marcus had completed most of the paperwork required for her discharge with the help of various cards from her wallet, so after just a couple of signatures, she was free to get going. She found Daniel and Dan sitting out in the hallway waiting for her, and after warm but gentle hugs and greetings, the group walked outside. The four of them piled into Marcus's truck, only just managing to squeeze in along the bench seat designed for three.

Daniel kept them all amused on the ride home with a mock review of the night from the attackers' perspective, from when they'd spotted "a couple of stunners" to when they'd admitted that they'd met their match "in the gay dynamic duo, who'd had just a dash of help from their new friend." Exhausted as she was, Lara would have been quite happy to stay squashed in there all night listening to Daniel's drivel, as it meant she was pressed firmly against Marcus's left side from shoulder to knee as he drove. And, judging by the less-than-subtle prod that she was receiving on her other side, Daniel was enjoying the seating arrangements as much as she was.

When they got to her and Daniel's house, Marcus walked around and helped them all out of the passenger door. The quiet groans as the three emerged signaled that they were going to know all about their injuries the next day.

"Well, thanks again, mate," said Daniel to Marcus, holding out his hand to shake. "Don't know what we would have done without you. I have many and varied talents, but brawling isn't one of them. How do you feel about becoming a gay icon? I can pretty much guarantee you'd be a big hit, with your looks. We'd just have to rustle up some bike shorts and sequins…"

"Yeah, thanks Marcus. Looking forward to seeing you again under less spectacular circumstances." Dan smiled, interrupting Daniel's nonsense. The two boys hugged Lara gently and wished her a comfortable night's sleep, before heading down the side of the house and disappearing. Lara turned to Marcus in the sudden stillness of the night. She drew an unsteady breath to calm the nerves that had just returned, and took his hand in her own.

"Well, words seem inadequate, but thanks, for everything. Yet again. You've gone well above and beyond the call of duty this time. For all of us."

"Are you kidding me? It was nothing…I'm just glad you guys are okay. I can't stop thinking about those brutes. If they'd hurt you any worse than they did, Lara, I swear to God…" She registered the tension in his body, while fighting the exhaustion in her own.

"But they didn't, thanks to you, and they've gone," she quickly placated him. "And all I want to do now is to go inside and have a hot shower and a long sleep. I can't wait to put this bizarre night behind me. Well, most of it, anyway…" She gave him a weak smile, and he looked back at her knowingly, lips pursed.

"Hmm. We sure are on some weird roller-coaster ride, aren't we? As I've said before, though, at least nobody could accuse us of being boring." He smiled. "All right, then. If you're sure, I'll come by here tomorrow. Or, later today, I guess I mean. In the meantime, I want you to ring me if there's anything you need. *Anything*. I programmed my number into your phone while you were sleeping. If you want me, I can be around here like a shot. Deal?"

"Deal," she agreed with a weary sigh, giving his hand a squeeze. "But there won't be any need. I'm getting sick of this 'damsel in distress' routine. It's really not my thing," she complained, and he chuckled quietly in response. As she made to head toward the house, though, he stopped her.

"Wait. Come here," he whispered, stepping forward and wrapping his arms around her slim body, pulling her into a tender embrace. She felt him breathing into her hair, before he kissed her gently on the top of her head. She allowed herself to lean into the comfort of his strong frame for one last minute.

"I'm just so glad you're okay," he whispered again with raw emotion, before pulling abruptly away and returning to his car. Lara sighed and made her way gingerly into the safety of her home, at long last.

Chapter 12

Lara slept deeply for the rest of the night, despite one nightmare about the brawlers, when she woke up crying out and lathered in sweat. Her head still ached when she finally arose after ten o'clock, but it was nothing that a dose of painkillers couldn't keep under control.

She turned on the cell phone that she hardly ever used and texted Pete, Kate, and Marcus, letting them know that she was fine, and laughed when she received Marcus's immediate response: *You're telling me. See you at 12:00 x.* Kate's return text expressed her sympathy and relief, but Pete remained silent, undoubtedly still asleep.

As she put the phone away in her bag, Lara heard voices from next door, before someone left the apartment and jogged down the stairs. Five minutes later, she heard an animated knock through the wall and grinned to herself. Making two extra strong coffees, she wandered into Daniel's apartment in her pajamas, dressing gown, and fluffy animal slippers. Daniel upstaged her completely in a black satin kimono with a dragon print across the back. He assessed her appearance disapprovingly.

"Well, you obviously didn't get lucky last night! God, girl, we've got to work on your wardrobe; it's really pathetic. You're making absolutely nothing of your God-given raw materials, and it's a crying shame. Exactly how do you expect to get across the line in toweling? And what's with those slippers? How old are you—twelve?"

"Nobody except you and my grandmother ever gets to see me in this get-up, Daniel, so I really couldn't care less." Lara laughed off his words, but glanced discretely in one of Daniel's several mirrors, and had to admit to herself that he had a point. She didn't look great.

"Honey, I'm going to make it a pet project of mine to make sure that someone special *does* get to see you in your night attire. Speaking of which…how about that guy of yours? Now I see what all the fuss is about! I was completely off base—you've got to hang in there…your taste is almost as good as mine!" Daniel smiled at her, obviously dying to talk about the developments with Dan.

"Soooo…" Lara asked obligingly. "Tell me!" And he did. Daniel's face shone with happiness as he described his conversations with Dan, during which they'd both admitted intense feelings for each other and decided to date exclusively. Dan had gone home this morning to change into some fresh clothes, but was returning later for dinner.

"I've got myself a Class A boyfriend, Lara," Daniel finished with a flourish. "And it feels AMAZING!" He jumped up from his chair as he sang out this last word, spinning around the room with arms flung wide, until the reality of his bruises kicked in, and he sat back down with a wince.

"Body not feeling quite as good as the spirit?" Lara asked.

"To tell you the truth, I've hardly noticed any pain. I've been floating three feet in the air with Dan. Who cares about such worldly matters?" said Daniel breezily. But then he looked at Lara more seriously.

"It wasn't too much fun last night though, was it? Enough to put you off being gay. Well, almost!" he continued lightly, before pulling her into a spontaneous hug. "Sorry you got caught up in such ugliness, my friend."

"Not your fault," she replied, giving him a gentle squeeze in return.

"Let me make it up to you anyway. French toast on me, coming up. Then I'm paying a visit to a little boutique I know to find you a black silky negligee for that extra special night-time occasion…"

Lara looked at him reprovingly.

"Trust me, it'll come in handy, and you'll be thanking me before you know it," he added with a wink. She gave a resigned laugh, before opening the newspaper, determined to enjoy the rest of the quiet Sunday morning.

*

Marcus knocked on her door not a minute after midday, looking no worse for wear after the trying night they'd all had. Somehow, he managed to look as good as ever in an old windcheater and torn jeans. Lara knew that the same couldn't be said about her, despite the half-hearted attempt she'd made to disguise her fatigued appearance with a bit of makeup, especially given the concentrated examination to which she was now being subjected.

"Hi. You don't look so hot," he concluded with a frown.

"Thanks for that," Lara retorted, and Marcus sighed theatrically.

"You know what I mean. How are you feeling?"

"A bit like I've taken a pounding in the surf on top of some concealed rocks, I must admit. But I'll live."

"Those bastards…"

"Hey, what's done is done. Let's not let it ruin the whole weekend, okay?" she pleaded. "I just want to put it all behind me now, and so does Daniel. Stuff happens. Then you get up, dust yourself off, and move on, you know?"

He observed her quietly for a few moments more, before giving in. "Okay. Good attitude. It's just that scum like that…"

"I know. But the law catches up with them eventually, remember? Finish your degree and throw the book at them that way, if you really want to do something useful. Until then, though, let's get some air." Lara grabbed her bag and they left her apartment, chatting about her morning with Daniel as they walked the few blocks to the local park. They sat down at a bench and just watched the local kids playing for a minute in companionable silence.

"Daniel's pretty keen on his new friend, then?" Marcus enquired conversationally.

"I'll say!" Lara laughed. "I've never seen him like this before. He's on cloud nine. I just hope he doesn't go and do anything over-the-top and put Dan off. But opposites can attract, of course, so hopefully Dan will just love him back for the kook that he is, and they'll be a raging success story." She took a sip from her water bottle, but nearly snorted the cool liquid back out when she heard Marcus's next words.

"What about you then, Lara? What sort of guys are you usually attracted to?" He regarded her levelly.

"What? I…I don't know what you…" Lara stammered, before glaring at him silently.

"Well, you told me once that I wasn't your type. I just wondered what it is you look for in a guy?" She searched his face for amusement, but it wasn't to be found. So she took a steadying breath and directed the spotlight back his way.

"That's not fair."

"What isn't?" He raised an eyebrow.

"You were the one who said we needed to talk about…things. You can't just put the onus on me to tell you about—stuff—like that." He observed her quietly for a minute.

"Okay. Maybe you're right," he said finally in a thoughtful voice, almost to himself. "But where to begin, in a conversation like this? Unknown territory."

At that, Lara leaned down to pat a wayward puppy, allowing him the time to gather his thoughts. It seemed to work.

"All right, here goes," he said eventually, after a deep exhalation, turning to her and speaking with unnerving directness. "Let the honesty session begin. Firstly, let me tell you something you already pretty much know. As your 'friend,' I'm shamefully, unspeakably attracted to you. I have been from the start." Lara couldn't breathe, let alone move a muscle.

"But physical attraction's usually pretty fleeting, in my experience, and it's not something I'd allow to get in the way of a good, longer-term friendship. So I put up a stop sign and kept those feelings for you on ice, as you know. And I've been playing a waiting game ever since, expecting the flame to flicker out. The problem is, it hasn't. Far from it," he added quietly, pausing to think while Lara swallowed apprehensively.

"Anyway, even though you made it quite clear where I stood with you a while back, *my* feelings have still been messing with the way I've been acting with you, Lara. I've been too friendly at times, like when we go out, and then I go and overcompensate and act all cool back at uni. It's so messed up. And I want you to know that I'm really sorry for all of the mixed messages I've been sending; I'm sure you're as fed up with this cat and mouse thing we've got going on as I am. In fact, probably more so, given that, from your perspective, the attention's no doubt been unwelcome." He sighed in frustration, regarding Lara levelly before continuing.

"The weird thing is that none of this is like the real me at all… I'm usually very controlled in my responses to people. Just not with you, it seems."

Lara stared at Marcus in silence, her mind racing ahead as she tried to work out exactly where his admissions were leading. All too soon though, she found out, and it was not in the direction she'd hoped.

"So…" he continued, while looking deeply into her eyes. "In a nutshell, it occurred to me last night that I needed to meet up with you away from everything and clear the air once and for all, so that we can take the heat out of the situation. You know, to 'reboot' our friendship and lose the tension I've added to it. What do you think?" He was watching her closely.

What did she *think*?

Lara's mind was all over the place, and she needed a minute to respond. On the one hand, she was thrilled and unnerved by Marcus's admissions of attraction to her. But his continued assumption that they should keep things between them platonic had her completely deflated, and she wondered whether it meant his feelings only ran skin deep. After all, when she really thought about everything he'd said, he'd only been talking about a physical connection, not an emotional one. And although she was completely inexperienced with the opposite sex, Lara knew that with some guys, that was as good as it got.

In short, she didn't know *what* to think, except that the time had come to move things forward, now that the opportunity had presented itself. She had to get in the game, and then find out exactly where she stood along the way. And so, calling on courage from within, she answered him in a low, clear voice.

"What do I think?" she repeated slowly. "Well, since you ask, what I think is that there are two of us sitting here, Marcus, and that you're only telling half of the story, if that. And, in my opinion, we have other options."

He paused for a long minute before responding. "Such as?"

"Such as getting together and giving things a shot."

Marcus's jaw tightened with her words, and his penetrating gaze could have pierced her soul. Lara started to panic. How much could he see about how she felt, despite her attempts to protect herself?

"I thought I wasn't your type," he said slowly.

"I lied."

"I see. I didn't realize." Another long pause. "I guess that changes things." His voice was husky and intense, and she shivered despite herself.

"So, you're feeling…?" He sought clarification.

"The same as you, it seems." Or possibly significantly more.

"Okay," he said, slowly. "I must admit, there've been times that

I've wondered about your reactions to me. But I thought I was just imagining things."

"You weren't."

"Right." He took a deep breath and closed his eyes, before leaning down to place his elbows on his knees and stare at the ground, apparently lost in thought.

After an agonizing minute, Lara broke the silence. "So where does that leave us, do you think?"

"Confused," he replied.

"Because…?"

"Because this is an unexpected complication."

"Oh, come on! It doesn't have to be all that difficult, does it? I mean, boy and girl meet, boy likes girl, girl likes boy. We're both young, free, and single. So maybe we should just do what other people do—go out on a date, even try some handholding or something…?"

No response.

"I mean, how hard can it be, Marcus?" Lara pushed on. "What've we got to lose, really? If we give things a try and they don't work out, I'm sure we can manage to dust ourselves off and stay civil, like grown-ups. And it's not like anyone else could get hurt…"

Silence.

Oh God, no. That was it.

"That is, assuming you're *available* for a relationship…" She forced herself to continue, her voice now noticeably strained. Once again, he failed to reply, and merely remained staring at the ground in front of him.

"Which, it seems, you're not…" Lara finished in a voice that was barely above a whisper. The situation had finally become clear to her; she'd put herself out there in front of the wrong guy, and it was going to backfire big time.

After an interminable minute, Marcus cleared his throat and sat up to face her, his expression heavy with regret. Lara, barely breathing, steeled herself for the bombshell she knew was coming.

"I'm so very sorry, Lara, but you're right. I'm not available for a relationship with you." And there it was, delivered in the strange, flat voice of a complete stranger.

Lara felt numb with shock. How had she not seen this coming? How had she misjudged this man so completely? It was *so* unlike her not to have read the play better than this…she must have been completely blinded by her infatuation. All she wanted to do was flee in embarrassment, but, taking a couple of shaky breaths, she forced herself to have it out with him, and replied.

"I see. Wow. So, let me get this straight…all this time, while you've been flirting away, and telling me, and God knows who else, that you're attracted to us, there's been someone else in the picture? You know what that makes you, don't you? That poor girl, whoever she is…"

"Lara, please, I didn't mean to hurt you in any way…" he began, a cocktail of emotions playing across his face as he spoke. But as he reached across to her in instinctive concern, she shook her head and waved him angrily away. She was already distancing herself from him—her body's way of protecting itself from pain.

"Just forget about it, Marcus," she snapped. "As far as I'm concerned, this conversation never happened. Whatever connection we might have had before is now meaningless, as far as I'm concerned. And there won't be any further 'complications' between us, don't worry. We're clearly on different planets when it comes to the bigger picture."

At that, Lara suddenly grabbed her bag and stood up without bothering to register the impact of her words. Her outburst finished, she could feel a wave of sadness approaching, and wanted to be well away from Marcus before falling in a heap. She had no interest in hearing another word out of his mouth, and she was damned if she was going to give him the satisfaction of seeing what he'd done to her.

"So I'll see you at uni, I guess," was all she managed to add over her shoulder, before striding away without so much as a backwards glance.

Uni, where they'd be back to being friends, at best.

Chapter 13

Back at university, Lara and her friends threw themselves into some serious study for the next three weeks. Essays were finalized and submitted, and then preparation began in earnest for mid-semester tests. Lara spent the majority of her weekday evenings in her favorite section of the now-busy law library, trying to cover all of the suggested reading when the necessary law reports weren't being monopolized by other students.

Although she would have preferred to steer clear of Marcus for good after discovering his deceit, she continued to attend their study group in light of the massive workload they faced, and for Kate's sake. It was too late in the piece to join forces with anyone else.

During the study sessions, the pair reached an unspoken agreement to continue treating each other exactly as they'd done before the gloves had come off—although it was all business, and no pleasure. And Lara discovered, to her relief that, with continued exposure to him, her initial fury and dismay had in fact largely abated, until she was once again mainly just relieved that their relationship hadn't become physical. Student life could continue along its well-trodden path, in spite of the private fire that had been ignited and acknowledged, and then blown up in her face. Their personal misstep was already ancient history.

When it came to studying for the criminal law test, Marcus joined Lara in the library from time to time, sitting at the desk next to hers and wading quietly through the material. Then, if one of them got stuck on a complicated judgment, they'd adjourn to a discussion room to review the topic at hand, although Lara drew the line firmly at shared coffee breaks. Marcus was obviously truly passionate about the subject, and together the two of them extracted threads of reasoning from the various precedents to prepare novel legal arguments accordingly.

Lara went into her test well prepared and thinking clearly, and worked her way through it with confidence. As she put down her pen at the end of the assessment, she looked across to where Marcus sat in the next row of desks as prescribed by the alphabetical listing, and raised her eyebrow. He winked in response and she nodded in return. They had both found it a walk in the park.

He was waiting for her outside once they'd all filed silently out of the room.

"Well done, partner. We make a formidable team!" he announced, and something inside her swelled, despite herself.

"It wasn't too bad at all, was it?" she replied as she moved away from the building.

"Very straightforward," he agreed. "But I'm *so* glad it's over. These mid-semester tests have been exhausting. How do you feel about celebrating this milestone over a bowl of pasta?"

"No, thanks." Lara kept on walking.

"Rrright. Can I ask why not?" He kept in step with her.

"I would've thought that was fairly obvious," she replied, rolling her eyes.

"Well it's not," he said. Lara stopped and looked at him incredulously.

"Because I don't want to hang out with you after our talk in the park, all right?"

"But haven't we been doing that regularly, while we've been studying?" He seemed genuinely bemused.

"I think the key words there are 'while we've been studying.' I can handle being your colleague, Marcus, if I don't think too hard about it. But I have absolutely no interest in being your friend." At that, Lara turned her back on him and continued to walk briskly along the path. After a minute though, she felt him reappear at her side.

"Ouch," was all he said.

"It's no more than you deserve."

"Maybe. But I still think you should join me for lunch."

Lara stopped in her tracks once again, now in a quiet courtyard between buildings. She was truly stunned at the guy's audacity. Was he so supremely confident of his hold over all women that he could just ignore a blatant rebuff? Or did he simply think she was playing a tantalizing game of hard to get? Time to make herself crystal clear, it seemed.

"Marcus," she started slowly. "I think you might be under a misapprehension about how I feel about you these days. It would be hard for me to put into words exactly how loathsome, how *repulsive* I find men who play around on their partners. The fact that you have a girlfriend, or whatever you call her, and yet you're standing here trying to convince me to go on some sort of date with you is beyond comprehension to me. It's really sick. To be frank, I—"

"Stop!" Marcus interrupted her forcefully, much to Lara's amazement, leaning toward her and holding her firmly by the shoulders as he did so.

"Let go of me!" she demanded, twisting her upper body in a failed effort to release herself from his grip. "How *dare* you!"

"Sorry, Lara, but you need to hear me out," he insisted.

"I really don't want to talk about your *relationship status*, or whatever it is you want to explain to me about your girlfriend, Marcus! I just want to get out of here, and—"

"There is no girlfriend," Marcus said quietly, but clearly.

Lara's heart skipped a beat. "You've broken up with her?"

"No. There never was one."

She stared at him quizzically, before giving a bemused shake of her head. "But you told me there was someone else."

"No I didn't. I told you I wasn't available to have a relationship with you."

Lara thought back to their ill-fated conversation, and realized that he was right. "Well, for God's sake, what on earth is *that* supposed to mean?" she blurted out.

"Only that I'm not interested in commitment right now. I've got too much on my plate already this year, and I don't know what's on the cards for me beyond that. I don't even know if I'll be staying in Melbourne past the end of this semester, at this point. So it doesn't feel right to throw something else—someone else— in the mix right now. I'd only let her—you—down, and it'd end in tears."

Lara's mind was reeling with this latest revelation, and it took her a minute to pull her thoughts together. "You've *got* to be kidding me," she said finally, her tone exasperated, but calmer. As her body lost its tension, he let go of her.

"I'm not."

"If that's all it was, then why didn't you just say so, Marcus? I'm a big girl; I could have lived with that explanation. And it sure beats believing you're a two-timing snake, and hating you for it. I don't understand why you let me walk away thinking that about you." She shook her head again, frowning in confusion.

"I'm not sure either, in retrospect." Marcus sighed. "It just seemed easier at the time, I suppose. I didn't want to have justify my lifestyle choice to stay single. I still don't. It just is what it is."

Lara thought about that for a couple of moments. "Just to clarify—you're not just making this 'lifestyle choice' so that you're free to experience all of the…err…*social opportunities* that university has to offer?"

"No, Lara." He sighed. "I know we don't know each other all that well, really, but that's not who I am. I'm a one-woman kind of guy. When I'm not determinedly single, that is."

"Okay," she concluded after another pause, wanting to question him further, but respecting his right to privacy and his right to choose. University was supposed to be about broadening your life experience, after all, and who was she to judge someone for having different values to her own? "Weird, but okay." A small smile now played on her lips.

"So, my 'monster' status has been rescinded? And you might even reconsider that bowl of pasta…?" He smiled back.

"Hmm. I'm still not sure, to be honest. You don't want a relationship, but it's all right to go out for lunch together? Kind of borderline, isn't it?" She wanted to know exactly where the line was drawn.

"Not at all," he replied. "After all, *friends* break bread all the time, Lara. Even friends who find each other fairly attractive. In fact, it's been known to happen even when one friend finds the other completely stunning." Marcus was grinning openly now, while Lara's heart was thumping oddly in her chest.

"Whatever happened to wanting to 'take the heat out of the situation?'" She blushed in response to his flirtatious remarks.

"That was back when I thought my attention was totally unwelcome, and it was necessary. Now, well, I can handle a little bit of warmth in the friendship, if you can. As long as we're clear on the boundaries, and you're okay with things this way," he clarified, his expression suddenly more serious.

Lara looked back at him thoughtfully, as she pondered his words. More than anything else, she was forced to acknowledge to herself just how much she was enjoying talking to him like this, and how much she'd missed their interpersonal connection. She wanted to be closer to him again, even if it didn't get them anywhere in the long run. So, maybe this was acceptable then— some innocent flirting on top of a friendship base. As long as she kept her defenses intact and didn't allow herself to hope for more, of course.

"Well, I guess it'd be nice to have a bit of a celebration, after all of our hard work." She smiled, answering all of his questions with that one statement. "So, I'm okay with it if you are, my *friend*. But let's eat upstairs here on campus, if you don't mind. It'll make it less weird."

"Great! It's a date," he replied lightly, as they started forward along the path once more, before giving her a sideways glance. "Or not."

And so the pair of them made their way to the student building and upstairs to the university's only semi-formal dining room. There, they took a window seat, talking all the while about the test paper. They compared responses, and confirmed that they'd been on the same track with their answers, to Lara's relief. When it came time to order, Lara screwed her nose up when Marcus selected a chinotto to have with his lasagna, and she chose a limonata instead.

"I don't know how you can drink that stuff," she commented. "It tastes like medicine."

"It's my favorite drink!" Marcus laughed at her disgusted expression. "What's yours?"

"Lemon, lime, and bitters," she replied.

"A safe choice. Favorite food?" he asked.

"Thai," she responded immediately, enjoying the easy banter they'd slipped into. "You?"

"Tiramisu," he said with a grin. "Which I intend to order for dessert, actually. Give me Italian, all the way."

They covered all of the big issues as they chatted: best and worst days (sporting thrills and fathers' deaths respectively for both of them), favorite places (mountains, beach), whether they were dog or cat people (both dog), and which famous personalities they'd ask to a dinner party ("definitely Matt Damon" being Lara's first pick, Nelson Mandela being Marcus's more mature choice). Then they got onto books, a shared passion, describing and contrasting their tastes at length as they polished off their meals, and promising to lend each other a couple of their favorite reads after the break.

Inevitably, though, after what seemed like such a brief moment in time, Lara looked at her watch and realized with a shock that more than two hours had passed since they'd sat down.

"Wow. How did that happen?" she wondered aloud.

"Well, you know what they say about time flying…" Marcus grinned. "Actually, I could sit here with you for the rest of the day quite happily. You're very easy to talk to."

Lara looked at him appraisingly. "How funny to hear you say that," she responded candidly. "I've always spent a lot of time on my own, and don't mix with people very easily. I'm usually only comfortable around people I've known forever, and am a bit of a social misfit with everyone else."

"You must've been hanging around the wrong people then," Marcus declared. "I don't think you and I'd ever get sick of each other. So just stick with me, kiddo, and I don't think we'll have too many dull moments!"

That sounded just fine to her.

"All right, I've really got to get moving," said Lara as she started to gather her belongings. "My grandmother's expecting me at the coast before nightfall, for a week of total relaxation before I have to head back. Not a textbook in sight. Sounds like bliss, doesn't it?"

"Sure does." He grinned as he settled the bill. "Although I was wondering if you'd be able to muster up enough energy to give this novice board-rider a surfing lesson on Sunday? I'm passing through Anglesea then before heading down to the Otway Ranges, and I thought it'd be a good chance to see you in action while I'm there."

For a few moments Lara was speechless, as she tried to visualize the picture he was painting. She wasn't completely sure how she felt about her two worlds colliding in this manner, especially after their recent turmoil. Excited, certainly, but confused as well.

"And how exactly would you describe such an excursion?" she finally brought herself to ask.

"I'd call it two friends catching up for a surf, Lara," he said slowly and clearly after a theatrical sigh. "Although possibly also a minor aberration, I suppose," he admitted after a pause.

"This is a strange game you're playing," she replied with a subtle shake of her head. "I can't seem to keep up with the rules."

"It's no game, believe me," he responded, his voice now quieter and more serious, and his expression grave. "I have no intention of messing with you, Lara. I'm not in the market for a girlfriend, as I've said, but that doesn't mean I don't want to spend a bit of time hanging out with you, if you feel the same way. I've missed you lately."

She didn't know what to say in reply, so she just busied herself getting up to leave.

"So, surfer girl, the ball's in your court," he continued in a more normal voice as they made their way out of the restaurant and down the stairs. "I'd love to join you out on the water, provided you take it easy on me, and can lend me a board. But I'll only come if you want me to, and you think it's appropriate. What do you think?"

Lara only had to consider his proposal for one second more, as they pushed through the front door of the building and stepped outside. She'd already made her decision.

"I think yes." She stopped and smiled shyly up at him.

"Excellent!" he retorted with a satisfied grin. "Guess I'll see you bright and early Sunday morning on your precious back beach, then. But just so you know, I'll be expecting you to join me for an activity in *my* comfort zone one of these days. I want to show off too. Fair's fair."

"Deal," Lara replied, trying to keep her emotions in check. "Can't wait."

"Me neither," he agreed, looking deeply into her eyes. "Until then, though…" He surprised her by pulling her into a gentle embrace and murmuring into her ear. "Mmmm, gotta love that tea rose."

And then he was walking away. She managed a faint goodbye and returned his wave, while inside she felt like she was melting. *This is up there with one of my better days*, she thought as she watched the back of him grow smaller in the distance. Then she floated home.

Chapter 14

On Sunday morning at Anglesea, after a restless night's sleep, Lara woke and smiled in anticipation of the day ahead. She carried an extra board down to the beach as well as her own in preparation for Marcus's visit, and saw that the surf was bigger than it had been during the previous couple of days when she'd been out. It was magic, and a couple of the local early birds were already out there taking full advantage. Lara paddled out and greeted them before riding the waves like a pro. She scanned the beach between sets, but searched for Marcus in vain. To her enormous disappointment, he remained a no-show as the morning went by. Then the breeze got up and the surf started to close in, so one by one the surfers rode in and disappeared, until she and Chief were left alone on the deserted beach.

Lara sat on the sand with an arm around her faithful companion and stared out at the horizon. She felt hollow and lonely inside, which forced her to recognize just how much she'd allowed Marcus's presence in her life to compensate for the previous void, despite the red flags. Which was entirely stupid. He wasn't a safe bet—in fact, he wasn't even in the race. He'd made that perfectly clear. Her attraction was making her weak, and that was something she despised. It had to be brought to a halt.

"Toughen up, girl," she said aloud to herself. "Dream time's over." Chief gave her hand a lick and she laughed cynically. "Come on then, boy," she said, standing to leave. "Let's get back to the real world."

It was to Lara's enormous surprise then that she found an old white pick-up parked in her grandmother's driveway. She made her way quickly around the back to dump the boards, towel herself off, and change into her windcheater and tracksuit pants. Then she entered the house through the back door, leaving her sandy Labrador outside to dry off. Inside, she was greeted with a surreal scene in which Marcus and Gran were sitting together at the kitchen table, chatting and laughing as they shared a pot of coffee and a plate of shortbread biscuits. Lara just stood at the door in stunned silence, while Marcus looked up at her in amusement.

"Look who's here!" announced Gran unnecessarily when she noticed Lara's arrival.

"Morning, surfer girl," Marcus greeted her. He looked drop-dead gorgeous in a cream cable-neck jumper and khaki cargo pants.

"I thought our arrangements were crystal clear?" she responded icily, ignoring his friendly tone.

"Aahh. You didn't get my text message, then," he observed, noting her obvious mood.

"I only have a cell phone for emergencies. I never use it," she replied sharply, still irritated.

"Well, that I didn't know. In which case, sorry I'm late," he countered. Lara remained standing in silence, weighing his reasonable tone against her morning's disappointment. Her grandmother wasn't going to allow her to remain bad-tempered, however. She got up and moved noisily around the kitchen, placing a third cup on the table with a bang and inserting two slices of bread in the toaster for Lara.

"Oh, stop your quarreling, you two. Lara, your friend has come all this way to see you, so put a smile on your dial and make him feel welcome, for goodness sake! I've got things to do in the garden. I told you, Marcus, she can be quite the handful." And with that embarrassing declaration and with a pointed look at Lara, she put her outdoor shoes on and disappeared out the back. Lara and Marcus looked at each other in silence for a couple of moments, before sharing a grin at Gran's rebuke.

"She's right. I'm sorry," said Lara, sinking into the chair next to his and pouring herself a much-needed coffee. "I was just really looking forward to sharing the beach with you this morning, and it was a let-down when you didn't arrive. You missed something special, you know."

"I know. I'm really disappointed too, believe me. I've been kicking myself the whole way down here. But on the plus side, I've had a great chat with your grandmother. She really is something," he said, shaking his head in wonder.

"Isn't she?" Lara agreed, but something was nagging at her. "What's she been telling you?"

Marcus grinned. "This and that. She's just been describing what you were like as a kid. You sounded adorable! Well, for the most part…"

Lara winced. "I'm guessing you got the 'hysterics at the circus' story." She sighed.

"And the 'wouldn't eat anything white' saga," he added.

"That's just great. Tell me, when do I get to meet your family and pry through all the skeletons in *your* closet?" But Marcus's expression closed, and he changed the subject.

"So have I completely missed the surf, then? Surely there's still something happening out there? It's not called the Surfcoast for nothing, is it?" he asked.

"No, but it's rubbish now the breeze has picked up," Lara replied. "It won't be any good until the tide turns back and the wind drops, at about four o'clock this afternoon."

"All right. Well, we'll just have to go out then, if it's still okay with you. Unless you have other plans?"

"You want to hang around here until then?" she asked, surprised but pleased.

"Absolutely! I'm not expected in Lorne until tonight, and I'm sure we'll think of some way to entertain ourselves in the meantime…besides, who knows what other interesting tidbits I might pick up about little Lara?"

"That would be *none*. Why are you so late, anyway?" Lara asked, buttering her toast and putting more bread in the toaster.

"I was out with Pete and Charlie last night," he replied, to Lara's surprise. "It was a big night."

"How big?"

"We caught two bands in St. Kilda and then moved on to a club in the city. I've had two hours sleep, and four cups of coffee already this morning."

"I see." She didn't want to judge him, but the picture he'd just painted didn't marry with his outdoor adventurer persona. The two lifestyles weren't complementary—at least not without something having to give. And that something, this morning, had been her.

"Again, Lara, I'm really sorry I let you down." He was watching her reactions closely. "Actually, I fully intended to get here at the appointed hour, but ended up being too tired to drive safely. It's my loss, I know." Lara decided to let it go, even though it sounded pretty lame. He did look regretful.

"Did you have fun out with those guys? Pete's great, but I can't see you and Charlie hitting it off particularly well…"

"Why do you say that?" Marcus asked, suddenly still.

"Because he's so obnoxious. Don't you find him an attention-seeking pain in the rear end?"

"I couldn't have put it better myself." Marcus smiled. "How well do you know him?"

"Only from watching the band from time to time. I never stick around afterwards. Clubbing isn't my thing, but even if it was, I couldn't stand hanging around and listening to his big-noting."

"So what do you think Pete sees in him?"

"They've just got the Burst connection, I think. I didn't realize they even went out together other than when they played," she said, getting started on her next round of toast and peanut butter.

"They were supposedly seeking musical inspiration last night, before we carried on to the club. I'm not sure how much was actually achieved though, given the state they were in. They were both totally wasted. Does Pete usually party that hard?"

"Well, he does love his beers, but I'm never around late enough to see exactly how messy he gets. He's never got any money left after going out though; that much I know. What's with all the interest in his personal habits, anyway?" she asked, once again reloading the toaster.

"Just curious." Marcus shrugged. "He's a good guy, I like him. Wow, how much more of that are you going to eat?" he asked, mesmerized.

"Hey, some of us have had a pretty active morning, out battling the elements, instead of just battling a hangover. Don't be rude!" she answered back defensively through her next mouthful. "Want some?" she pointed to the bread.

"No thanks. I had a hotdog with all the trimmings only a few hours ago…" They gave each other simultaneous looks of revulsion, then laughed.

"So then, if you're sticking around, what are you up for?" Lara asked after a while, rising to clear away the dishes. "I can offer you a walk on the beach with my hound, or Scrabble by the fire, or fishing…"

"Hmm. Good selection. Well, I choose fishing, for starters, if you've got enough gear for both of us. Provided you've finished feasting, of course…"

She flicked a tea towel at his shoulder from her vantage point, satisfied with the yelp she elicited. Laughing, the two of them went out into the back garden, where Marcus received a slobbery welcome from Chief after a brief sniffing interlude.

"He's just like my family's old dog, Yeti, except black instead of golden!" he exclaimed with pleasure. Having knelt down for some serious petting, Marcus grabbed the dog's chewed-up, old tennis ball and threw it toward the back of the garden a few times, much to Chief's delight. The ferocity of his wagging indicated that, as far as the dog was concerned, Marcus was a friend for life.

Meanwhile, Gran indicated that she felt the same, from the edge of the lawn where she was weeding a flowerbed.

"Handsome, charming, *and* well-mannered," she whispered, so that only Lara could hear. "Your boyfriend's got my stamp of approval! Good taste, sweetheart."

"He's not my boyfriend, Gran," Lara hissed back.

"Well, he should be! Maybe it's time for you to do something about that!" the old woman insisted, louder this time. Lara thought she saw the corners of Marcus's mouth lift slightly, and she blushed in embarrassment.

"Come on, let's get out of here, now that you've won over my entire family," she instructed him curtly, pursing her lips as his half-hidden smirk became an openly proud grin. She took two surf-casting rods, a well-stocked tackle box, a bucket, and some frozen whitebait from the shed and, after receiving Gran's instructions to bring back enough fish for dinner, they made their way toward the track over the sand dunes with Chief. At the top, Marcus stopped to appreciate the enormous view.

"Wow, this is spectacular!" he exclaimed. "No wonder you love coming here so much, with this right at your doorstep…it's heaven on earth!"

Now it was Lara's turn to enjoy a sense of pride. She'd instinctively known he'd appreciate the raw beauty of the place.

The pair made their way to the ocean's edge and walked along for a couple of minutes until they reached a spot near some rocks where Lara had regularly caught salmon. Then they both got busy baiting their rods and wading out into the water, pants rolled up, to cast their lines as far as possible toward the deeper, calmer water where the fish were likely to be lurking. They had to stand a distance apart in order to ensure that their lines didn't tangle, so talking wasn't an option other than when they came back to replace lost bait. But the silence was peaceful and companionable, both of them relaxing with their thoughts. Then, when Lara was the first to reel in a decent-sized fish, Marcus came over and whistled his approval.

"Hey, you're not too bad at this," he smiled, with a teasing look. "For a girl."

Her eyes flashed. "Is that so?" she asked. "Let's see just how 'not too bad' I can be, then, shall we?" The challenge was on. Lara was determined to show him up, despite his obvious experience casting a rod. She was momentarily elated when she caught another salmon, but it was undersized, and had to be thrown back. Then, to her annoyance, her line snagged and she lost her sinker, necessitating some fast repair work with deft fingers and fancy knot tying. Her skill was not lost on Marcus though, who watched her work with a raised eyebrow and a grin.

"At least I'm on the scoreboard, which is more than I can say for some," she crowed, although was more subdued when he landed a much larger fish than hers only half a minute later. And so they continued to fish in earnest, bringing in a good catch between them, until about an hour later, when Lara reeled in a feisty crab that had gotten stuck on the line by mistake.

"Doesn't count." Marcus laughed, as she tried to dislodge the critter, which was waving its enormous nippers threateningly toward her every time she got close. "Here, allow me to assist," he continued, putting his own rod aside and helping to untangle its various wriggling legs, careful to approach it only from behind to avoid getting bitten. Finally, he got the creature free and put it near the water's edge, where it quickly dug its way back to safety.

"All right, I concede," said Marcus, looking into the bucket and doing a headcount, before holding his hands up in the air. "Enough's enough. You win the hunting and gathering award for today, even though that's supposed to be *my* job. You mustn't have read the memo." Lara laughed at his nonsense as they packed up the gear and started back toward the house.

"You smell revolting," she told him with a wrinkled nose as they walked up the path next to each other.

"Right back at you, sweetheart." He smiled. "If I didn't think that a woman who knows how to rig and bait her own line is about the sexiest thing in the world, you'd be completely grossing me out right now! But as it happens, I'll probably be seeing you again in this hideous state in my dreams tonight. So it's been well worth it."

"I'll bet you use that line on all the girls," Lara replied dryly.

"You'd be surprised how few girls would be caught dead anywhere near fish guts," he said.

"Right," she retorted.

"And how absolutely compelling you are in comparison," he continued in a different tone. She couldn't look at him, and they continued home in silence, other than Marcus quietly humming the Hoodoo Gurus' song "Bittersweet" to himself.

Back at the house, Marcus filleted the fish near the drain in the back garden while Lara went in to wash, scrubbing herself repeatedly with soap to remove every trace of *eau de salmone*. Then it was his turn, and he came out fresh and clean, having changed into jeans and a navy shirt from the back of his car, his feet remaining bare. They sat down to enjoy a bowl of hearty vegetable soup and crusty bread with Gran, before settling down around the fire for a rest. Gran turned on the radio in the corner of the living room and relaxed back in her easy chair to enjoy some mellow jazz with her weekend crossword. Lara sat at the table and read the Sunday papers, while Marcus promptly fell asleep stretched out on the couch, Chief at his feet. The scene could not have been more typical, or more unusual, for that little house on a weekend.

Chapter 15

After about an hour, Marcus awoke, horrified that he'd fallen asleep in Gran's house during the day.

"Well, you can make it up to me by fixing a couple of things around the place before you two head out, if you're at all handy," Gran told him. Then he was promptly put to work up a ladder fixing a stuck window, re-attaching an air-conditioning vent that had come loose, and replacing some old globes inside and out, while Gran followed him around issuing detailed instructions, much to his amusement. Lara smiled and let them be, heading out the back to wax her boards. When she returned, Marcus was just finishing his allocated chores, and Gran was preparing to go out.

"Thank you, Marcus; they're the main things I needed done. We're not too fond of heights around here, as you might've guessed. Now you two go off and have some fun before it gets too late." But Marcus was crouching down at the back door.

"I think someone needs to take a look at these old steps, Mrs. Lees. Apart from the fact that they're not even close to level, the wood's almost rotten through. Have you thought about replacing them with a brick structure?" But Gran only waved her hand at him dismissively.

"Watch what you're saying, young man! Those steps are not as old as I am, and they've got character. I didn't ask you to start redesigning my home now, did I? So, off you go now. Go on." Duly dismissed, Marcus walked out the front with a shrug, an uncertain frown still on his face.

Lara returned to the shed and changed back into her damp wetsuit, shivering as she did so. Then, walking around the front of the house with a board under each arm and a towel around her neck, she interrupted Marcus standing by his truck. He was pulling his own tight neoprene suit up his legs and over his bathers, but was stripped bare from the waist up. When he straightened and looked at her, Lara simply stopped and stared at him. The sight of his strong brown shoulders, sprinkling of dark chest hair, and lean waist and stomach literally took her breath away. Clothed, he was beautiful; naked, he was sublime. How was it that this magnificent man was standing like that in her garden?

She could see immediately that Marcus had registered her unguarded desire. But rather than turning away to ignore and defuse the ticking time bomb as she'd expected him to, he surprised her by merely standing motionless, granting her silent permission to look her fill. His own eyes transmitted a very mixed message: anxiety and reluctance, but also a deep, undeniable longing of his own. Then he took a deep breath and closed his eyes for a minute with a tiny frown, before opening them again and allowing time to recommence.

"This isn't part of the plan, Lara," he said in a husky voice.

"I know," she replied quickly. "I'm sorry."

"Don't be. I'm the one who's put us in this position, by coming here. I should've known where it could lead." He took a breath, and then exhaled deeply, before reaching to pull up the remaining half of his wetsuit and continuing in a lighter tone.

"Time to get back with the program now, though. We're going surfing, remember? I think a dousing in the freezing cold water is exactly what we both need. Come on!" he said, taking one of the boards from under her arm and giving her a gentle push toward the track after grabbing his own towel. At that, her feet started moving obediently, and they walked toward the water without talking, lost in their own thoughts and feelings.

*

The shock of the ocean's early spring bite brought Lara back to her senses the second she set foot in the water. It was so icy that even Chief seemed disgusted, turning tail after a few seconds and walking up to the dry sand to lie and watch the crazy humans. Although there was not another soul in sight, the waves were a nice size, just about right for a beginner surfer to get a good ride. Marcus turned to Lara with a grin.

"This is going to be awesome," he said. "But remember, I've only been out a couple of times. You'll have to show me how it's done. And please restrain all laughter, however justified it may be, and rescue me if I get into any trouble!"

"You'll be fine," she encouraged him. "Just stick near me and don't let yourself drift downwind too far. Remember there are rocks about twenty meters along."

She waded out a few steps before lying down on the board and starting to paddle out beyond the break. Marcus followed, making light work of this strenuous activity with his superior arm strength. Once they started catching waves though, it was obvious that Lara was the more experienced and skilled surfer, moving her small board down and across the waves like an expert despite the morning's exertions. Marcus yelled out his praise and encouragement, evidently unconcerned about being trumped by a female in a sporting endeavor.

For his part, although clearly a novice who initially copped a pounding in the white water, Marcus's natural balance and athleticism enabled him to ride the waves in nicely once he got the hang of standing up quickly enough on the board. Judging by his wide-eyed concentration and the exultant whoops when he got moving, he was clearly exhilarated with his effort and achievement, and Lara was proud of him too.

After about an hour of activity though, the water temperature got to them both and they headed back to the empty, barren beach. There, Lara towel-dried her face and hair before stripping her wetsuit off to waist level. She wrapped the towel around her shoulders, so that it hung loosely over her one-piece bathing suit and protected her from the early evening chill.

As she turned back to where Marcus stood a couple of meters away, she noticed that he'd also stripped back down to waist level, had rubbed his hair semi-dry and was standing watching her with crossed arms, his towel flung carelessly over one shoulder. All she could see in his eyes this time was hunger. And all she could do was stare back at his muscular beauty in return for a long, long minute, while the world around them disappeared. Finally, inevitably, he approached, step by deliberate step, gaze unbroken.

"So, our moment of reckoning has arrived, Lara," he said quietly. "And this is crazy, and all wrong, but I forfeit."

"Meaning?" Lara managed to ask, with a swallow.

"Meaning, I can't take this anymore," he said with a crack in his voice as he stood directly in front of her. "Meaning, you're so unbelievably beautiful." He reached up with both hands and combed her damp hair back from her head with his fingertips, repeating the movement several times until he held it in a bunch at the nape of her neck. "Meaning, I ache for you," he whispered roughly as he suddenly released her hair and pulled her body tightly against his own, sending shivers down her spine.

"Oh God, Lara," he breathed into her ear, "tell me this is okay with you, even though it doesn't change things…tell me that we can have this one perfect day, even if it doesn't go any further…"

In reply, she merely pulled ever so slightly back so she could look up into his eyes, gazing at him with a desperation that matched his own. Finally, they'd found their way to each other, as she'd always hoped they would. Slowly, she raised a hand and traced a finger across his perfect, cool lips, stunned that she had the right to do so. And that was Marcus's undoing.

He groaned involuntarily and shuddered as he surrendered to their mutual desire, before leaning into her without any further hesitation. Their lips made contact with an electrical charge, shocking Lara with the intensity of the sensation. Their kiss, once it began, was passionate and frantic, each of them furiously exploring the tastes and textures of the other. Salt, spice, sweetness. Tongues, teeth, ragged breath. Hands held tightly around each other, grasping, their body heat counteracting the freezing cold air.

Then, after a minute, a calmness of sorts descended and the kiss softened, becoming tender and warm. Fingertips explored faces and necks, gently touching, stroking each other. A sigh from him, a gentle moan from her. Wonderment and relief.

Eventually, though, after an eternity, their lips moved a fraction apart, and they simply breathed together and stared into each other's eyes until their racing pulses slowed, their mutual need temporarily satiated. Then Marcus tilted his head and kissed Lara softly on each temple, before holding her chin in one hand and stroking her cheek with his thumb. The awe she felt was reflected in his own expression.

"Wow," he said coarsely, after clearing his throat. "That's some pretty heady stuff."

"Just give me a minute to come back down to earth," she replied shakily, before continuing a few moments later. "You're very, very good at that."

"That wasn't me. That was us, believe me. Sometimes things just work."

"I guess so," she said, surprising herself by picking up the hand on her face and kissing his palm until she felt him quiver. "I'm not sure quite where it leaves us though."

"God only knows, Lara," Marcus replied with a small frown, pulling her gently into his warm embrace, protecting her from the wind as he kissed her on the forehead. "Could we just quarantine today, consider it an anomaly, do you think? Enjoy what we have left of it, without worrying about the future?"

"Agreed," she said with a sigh, willing herself not to want more, or to question why she couldn't have it. He'd been consistent and clear about his boundaries from the start, after all.

"You sure? I don't want you to resent this later."

"I won't." She reached up to kiss him softly on the cheek, but as her lips moved toward his mouth, he turned his head to the side, resisting her temptation with obvious reluctance.

"Come on, let's get you home first. You're turning blue." He smiled, tucking a lock of damp hair behind her ear. Grudgingly, she agreed. Despite the heat she felt inside, her body was frozen and her feet were actually numb. After giving her cheek a final stroke, Marcus reached to pick up both boards and they started briskly up the track with Chief.

"What an absolute rush it was out there," Marcus said conversationally as they went, in an attempt to bring them back to reality. "No wonder you're such a surf junkie…that was awesome! And you're spectacular on a board," he added admiringly.

"You're not so bad yourself," she replied, trying to inject a tone of normality into her voice. "It took me months to get to the level you're at. You're obviously a natural. Is there anything you actually do badly?"

"Lots of things." He grinned. "My cooking's pretty average. I'm hopeless at cards. And golf…I lack the necessary patience. Plus I can barely manage to draw a stick figure," he answered honestly. At least he was human. "You?"

"Directions," she replied. "I'm the worst. That's one of the reasons that I don't have a car. I'd be permanently lost."

When they'd reached Gran's place and stowed their boards in the shed, Lara disappeared inside for a quick, hot shower and changed back into her jeans, and then Marcus did the same while she made a pot of steaming tea. Gran was out visiting a friend until dinner time, according to the note she'd left stuck to the fridge, so they had the place to themselves for a bit. A thought that thrilled and terrified Lara at the same time.

When he re-emerged from the bathroom, Marcus stoked the embers in the fireplace and added more wood until a cheerful blaze warmed the room once more. The pair of them lit the lamps and sat on the couch drinking their tea as dusk fell. They held hands intermittently and chatted about Marcus's pending hike with his friend Tim and Lara's plans for the week ahead. From time to time, they just leaned against the back of the couch in silence and watched each other, smiling, reveling in their newfound closeness, however temporary it was to be.

Marcus occasionally reached across to brush the back of his hand gently across Lara's cheek, and at one point, she kissed his fingertips when they strayed too close to her mouth, enjoying the effect on his expression. But by unspoken agreement, neither of them allowed the mood to become more passionate. They were conscious of being in Gran's house, and knew that if they started down that path again, it would in all likelihood be impossible to stop.

"So will you stay with us for an early dinner?" Lara asked after a time. "You did catch it, after all, caveman."

"I'd love to." He smiled in return. "Let's get it organized." They got busy in the kitchen, Marcus dusting the fish fillets with flour, pan frying them in butter, and cutting some lemon wedges, while Lara made some homemade fries and a simple green salad. Marcus was just setting the table for three and pouring them some white wine when Gran returned.

"Excellent!" she exclaimed. "I'm starving! And I'm so glad you're joining us, Marcus. It's nice to have some male company around the place for a change." They sat down as Lara served, and raised their glasses for a toast. "To friendship and beyond," announced Gran with her usual subtlety, and the three of them clinked glasses with looks of amusement, embarrassment, and mischief respectively. As they ate the simple but tasty meal, Gran chatted about her visit with the various neighbors, while Marcus asked her polite questions, seemingly genuinely interested in getting to know the older woman better. After a while, Gran looked at him searchingly.

"How old are you, young man?" He looked down at his plate and scooped up his last mouthful of salad before replying.

"Twenty-four, ma'am. I didn't settle into study until a couple of years after finishing school. So I'm a bit older than most of the other second year graduates."

"Twenty-four, you say?" said Gran thoughtfully. "You have the social graces of someone older. Huh!"

He shrugged in reply. "Well, Lara's not exactly immature either, Mrs. Lees."

"Good point," she agreed. "And do you work, as well as studying?"

Fair question, thought Lara, interested in his response. She remained curious about whether he was earning any kind of living these days; surely a student's savings couldn't see him through indefinitely?

"Not right now," he answered her, before looking at Chief and leaning down to give him a pat.

"Then how do you afford to rent your own apartment in inner-city Melbourne?" Gran asked somewhat nosily. "They're not exactly cheap."

"I saved money before I started the course, and so far it's been enough to keep me going," Marcus replied sketchily. "Speaking of real estate, what are the property prices like around here at the moment? Has the coastal market been as badly affected by the economic downturn as the cities?" he asked, deftly changing the subject. Gran was only too happy to launch into one of her favorite topics, which lead on to how the region had changed in general over recent years.

Lara reached under the table and took Marcus's hand, giving it a squeeze to acknowledge his discomfort about the personal line of questioning. He returned the squeeze and kept hold of her hand, his thumb rhythmically stroking the back of it as he talked and listened. Lara just sat and let the conversation move on around her, enjoying his touch and loving having him here in her family home. How quickly things could change.

*

After they'd finished eating and cleared away the dishes, the three of them sat down with a second glass of wine for a ferocious game of Scrabble. Gran was an old hand and an addict, and Lara dared Marcus to try to beat her. It soon became apparent though that her grandmother was completely dominating the game. Marcus looked at the woman admiringly, and then seemed to direct his efforts toward creating a sub-text to the evening. He smiled across at Lara after managing to spell "BEACH," but only raised a subtle eyebrow when his next word was "DESIRE."

"Double score!" exclaimed Gran, busy adding up his total and writing it down.

"Not yet," he murmured quietly to Lara in response, a comically suggestive expression flashing briefly across his face. Lara blushed and looked away.

When Gran had annihilated them with her final score, Marcus pronounced her the undisputed champion, but reserved the right to redeem himself another time in a different pursuit. They agreed on backgammon, before Marcus leaned back and stretched, looking at his watch and sighing.

"Well, ladies, duty calls! It's time for me to take my leave, and put this fabulous day behind me. I've got an old buddy to meet and a campsite to set up before a ridiculously early start heading into the mountains tomorrow. Many, many thanks, Mrs. Lees, for welcoming me into your beautiful home. It's been a real pleasure."

"You just make sure you come back soon, you hear?" Gran

replied, as they stood up and pushed their chairs in. She surprised Lara by giving their visitor a spontaneous hug, and seemed to say something quietly into his ear before turning to her armchair and the television.

"Right-o," said Marcus with a deep breath, leaning down to give the prostrate Chief one final scratch of his tummy. "It's been nice to meet you too, mate." Then Lara walked him out the front door and down to the drive on her own, until they stood once more by his truck. There she stood, hugging her arms across her chest, protecting herself from the darkness and the cold.

"What did Gran just say to you?" she asked Marcus curiously.

He paused before answering. "She told me to take good care of you." He sighed. "And so this is where I start beating myself up, because that's not where this is going. I've been as weak as water today and given in to all of these…incredible, indescribable feelings, when I should know better."

"Don't do that," she urged, louder than she'd intended. "Let's not have any regrets about today. We've already established that this is just a short-term fix…it's not like you haven't been up front about that. And, don't worry—if I'm not happy, I'll walk. You'll be the first to know, if that happens."

"Okay, then. Agreed." Although she detected some hesitation beneath the surface when he spoke, he smiled gently at her, and brushed his hand across her cheek. "You're incredible. And I want you to know something, Lara. This has been one of the best days of my life. I'll never forget it." He pulled her into his arms, drawing her close to him in the cold night air so she could feel his heartbeat and breathe in his potent, musky smell.

"I concur, counselor," she replied, before leaning forward to kiss him on the mouth. With a surprised groan, he gave in to their undeniable magnetism once more, pulling her face roughly back to his own. They picked up where they'd left off a few hours earlier, instinctively responding to each other as if they'd been connected for a lifetime. They kissed deeply and passionately for several long, breathless minutes, arms wound tightly around each other.

Finally though, when the tension had built to an almost unbearable level, Marcus broke the kiss, and they simply stood in each other's arms, struggling for control. It was some time coming, though; their bodies were pressed together from head to toe in an embrace that was supposed to cool their fervor, but was tantalizingly intimate. Lara couldn't think straight, and nor apparently could Marcus.

"Good God, I'm going to drive the truck straight off a cliff if I don't get a handle on this!" He laughed shakily, still breathing heavily as he extricated himself carefully from her arms.

"Take care out there. I'll miss you," Lara replied quietly, feeling his absence already.

"Me too," he said, his face serious. "I won't be contactable during the week, but I'll see you soon, surfer girl," he said, stepping forward to give her another quick hug and a warm kiss on the mouth.

Then, with a final goodbye, he got into the car and reversed, steadfastly refusing to look back at her. His hand waved out of the window as she watched his taillights moving away along the road, until he turned a corner and disappeared. She sighed with a mixture of happiness and resignation, before going back inside to her family.

Chapter 16

The following Sunday evening, just before university was due to start back, Lara was enjoying some quiet music and preparing to open a bottle of sparkling wine alone in her Melbourne apartment when there was a knock at the door. Surprised, she walked across the room and peered through the keyhole, only to see Marcus's magnified features in the framed circle. She opened the door, stunned.

"What are you doing here?" she blurted out incredulously.

"Umm, I'm not exactly sure." He shuffled uncomfortably. "Is it a bad time?"

"No, but…" Lara couldn't finish the sentence, unnerved by this unannounced visit.

"I can go if you'd like." He'd observed her discomfort. "But, just so you know what you'll be missing, I come bearing gifts." He held up a plastic bag obviously full of takeaway food. "It's Thai. Rumor has it that you're a fan."

"Thai? Oh, well, in that case, you'd better come in," she finally decided, motioning toward the table that was adorned with a vase full of multi-colored garden roses, before shutting the door behind him. "To what do I owe this unexpected pleasure, though? I thought you were still away."

"Well, I decided to cut the trip short so I could say happy birthday to a certain twenty-two-year-old girl." He grinned in response to her look of bemusement as he set the food on the table.

"Kate told me before the break. Which was greatly appreciated, since you obviously didn't see fit to share such salient details with me…hey, nice flowers. They're from your grandmother's garden, I take it? They smell like you, to the best of my recollection. Come here and let me check." He surprised her again by reaching out and wrapping his arms around her, breathing deeply and sighing. "Mmm, yep."

As before, the feeling of being held by him was overwhelming and addictive. But, after a few moments, Lara forced herself to pull back, needing time to get used to the change in atmosphere.

"Should we have dinner?" she suggested to divert the conversation. "I'm famished."

"Good idea." Marcus grinned and gave her hand a squeeze. "Let's get into this food while it's still hot."

Lara popped the wine cork and filled two flutes with the golden, bubbling drink, while Marcus found plates and chopsticks and opened up the various boxes he'd brought. It looked and smelled delicious.

"So, here's cheers!" Lara announced, raising her glass once they'd sat at the table.

"Cheers!" Marcus replied as they clinked glasses. "And happy birthday, beautiful." Lara blushed at the endearment. "What've you done with the day, anyway?"

"I went to the National Gallery with Daniel and Dan, actually. Not that I know much about art. But it was great, really relaxing." She went on to describe some of her favorite paintings between mouthfuls of the delicious dinner.

"Over to you, then. How was your hike?" she asked, changing the subject as she helped herself to some coconut curry.

"It was fantastic." He told her about the tracks and streams, the ancient flora and fauna of the Otways as they ate. "It really is one beautiful stretch of untouched wilderness. I can't wait to go back and see some more of it. I'm going to try and make a longer trip at the end of this year when uni's finished."

"Maybe we could go together?" Lara asked hesitantly, but Marcus only looked at her for a few moments in silence, much to her embarrassment. Then he moved the conversation on as if she hadn't spoken, before eventually wiping his mouth with a serviette, leaning back in his chair, and sighing. Lara pushed her plate away as well.

"Right, now we're at the business end of the evening," he declared, refilling their glasses and standing up. "Let's adjourn to the drawing room." This announcement was accompanied with a grand sweep of his arm toward the couch, not two meters from where they'd been sitting.

Lara smiled and settled back against the soft cushions with her legs curled underneath her, enjoying the warmth from the radiant heater and Marcus's outstretched arm across her shoulder as she sipped her drink.

"So. About your birthday present," he began.

Lara sat up expectantly. "Present?"

Marcus smiled. "Thought that'd spark your interest! Typical woman, out for whatever you can get..." he joked.

"Gimmee," she responded deadpan, holding out her hand. Marcus reached into the pocket of his discarded jacket and pulled out another bag, which contained a small parcel wrapped in black tissue paper. She opened it to find a delicate silver charm bracelet, already adorned with a single charm: a surfer on a tiny silver board, knees bent and arms outstretched. It was exquisite, and she looked up at him, speechless.

"I thought you could collect different charms whenever you travel to new places, and add them to that one," he explained as he fiddled with the catch and placed it on her wrist, "but that the surfer would always remind you of home."

She held her hand out in front of her to inspect his gift in its place, struggling to keep her emotions under control. "It's perfect. I'm going to wear it as my good luck charm. Thank you," she finally managed to say, still choked up by his generosity and thoughtfulness.

"You're welcome, surfer girl." Marcus smiled in return.

"I still don't understand what I am to you," Lara found herself whispering, and the look on his face softened and deepened.

"What are you?" he responded gently, reaching up to brush a strand of hair off her face. "You're a woman who makes complete sense to me. Whose company I crave, because she makes every experience better. Someone I just can't stop coming back to, even though I should know better."

As Lara absorbed his heartfelt words and the conflict in his beautiful eyes, a slow warmth spread through her body. And, for once, she was absolutely sure about what would happen next. Like a well-choreographed dance routine, she and Marcus leaned slowly, ever so slowly, closer until their mouths connected in a feather-like kiss, their arms slipping softly around each other. At first, Lara's lips moved gently in response to his, while they both readjusted to the shift in circumstances and the remembered sensations. Then, when her mouth opened a little, she heard a small moan escape his throat, and her breathing quickened as she felt his body shudder involuntarily.

From that moment, Marcus took control. His hold around her tightened as he pulled her even closer in toward him, his tongue demanding access to her mouth, which she granted immediately. His sudden urgency matched her own, and it thrilled her to the core. The heat between them flared more powerfully than ever as they kissed each other with unguarded passion for endless, silent minutes. The intensity was overwhelming, and she could see her own wildness mirrored in his bright eyes.

"Oh, Lara, Lara," Marcus whispered, breaking away to cover her face with kisses before returning feverishly to crush her mouth, his hands stroking her throat and neck, sending shivers down her entire body. For her part, Lara felt as if she were quenching a desperate thirst. She ran her hands repeatedly through his hair, and then kneaded his strong shoulders, before eventually reaching underneath his top and allowing her fingers to roam across the hot, smooth skin of his back. The direct contact with his body was electrifying, and he gasped before pulling forcefully away, staring at her. It was all she could do not to hold out her hands and beg… she ached for him.

"I'm afraid we need to hold it there, sweetheart," he finally managed to say, his hands holding her own between them, gently but firmly. "I can only keep things on track if we set boundaries and do our best to stick to them. Please, believe me, it's in both of our best interests in the long run." His over-bright eyes pierced into hers, imploring her to understand. But to understand what, that was the question.

"I'm not quite sure where you're drawing the line," she said, her voice shaking slightly. "But I think you're talking about trying to hold back the tide."

"Maybe so. But I'm pretty strong, and so are you."

"No one's strong enough to stop a tidal surge," she replied, raising a disbelieving eyebrow before continuing. "So, let me get the rules straight. We can be together, sometimes, as long as we're chaste, but maybe only for the short term. Wow, you really know how to sweep a girl off her feet, you know that?" She couldn't keep the edge out of her voice.

Marcus looked at her searchingly for a minute. Then his expression softened and he sighed, before responding quietly.

"Lara, I can leave, if this middle ground is getting too weird for you. I probably shouldn't have come in the first place. I just seem to be having a lot of trouble staying away."

"No, don't leave." She shook her head insistently.

"Meaning you're comfortable with the status quo?"

"Meaning I *think* so," she answered slowly, but less sure than she'd been a week ago, now that reality was sinking in. "Depends whether you're asking my head or my heart, I guess. And on whether this is all it can ever be."

There was a lengthy pause before he replied in a halting, careful tone. "I'm really sorry, but I can't answer that, Lara. My future plans are totally up in the air, as I've already told you, so I can't make any promises."

"I know," said Lara quietly, subdued by this reminder of what an unsafe bet he was. But at least he was being honest, and at least it wasn't an outright rejection. She looked at him for another minute with indecision.

"Not sure?" he asked, reading her expression.

"My mind's all over the place," she confessed with a weak smile.

"Well, let me know as soon as you've sorted it all out, all right? In the meantime, why don't you come here?" he murmured, holding out his arm. After a brief hesitation, Lara complied. He pulled her gently into his muscular chest, and lay against him, listening to the strong beat of his heart, while he rhythmically stroked her hair. Now and then, he leant down to kiss her on the top of her head, responding to private thoughts he didn't feel the need to share.

Oh, who was she kidding? This was heaven. And, provided she was prepared to walk at the first sign of trouble, she could accept it.

"Okay, I concede," she told him, once she'd made up her mind. "This is enough."

"This is a whole lot," he corrected her, and his hold around her tightened. And there the two of them lay for an age, peaceful, warm, and happy in their tiny, private world. Lara thought dreamily that she felt like she was floating, or flying, and the out-of-body sensation was simply beautiful.

Eventually though, she sat up and yawned.

"So, my *friend*, given the limited options, how does coffee and chocolate in front of a tame DVD sound? Possibly with a bit of handholding? That was my plan before you arrived, so if you want to join me for my electrifying birthday celebration, you'd be more than welcome."

"Sounds perfect. What movie's on offer?" Marcus asked, his body relaxing with the change in mood. He grinned when she reached across and held up *The Bourne Supremacy*. "Matt Damon. Should have guessed. You won't go getting all excited on me again now, will you? There's only so much temptation this poor, helpless man can take."

"I can't give you any guarantees, sorry. But I'll do my best to keep it decent, if you absolutely insist."

"Then it's a deal." He smiled.

As they stood up to get organized, Marcus surprised Lara by wrapping his arms around her once more. "Thanks for your understanding," he said into her ear. "It's more than I deserve."

"No problem." She smiled. "For now." He just looked deeply into her eyes and kissed her gently on the forehead in silent reply, before heading to the kitchen to turn on the kettle.

Chapter 17

Back to uni, back to their friends, back to normal. Their rendezvous during the break might never have happened, Lara thought to herself, as she and Marcus went about their usual routine. On again, off again; up a ladder, down a snake. Which kept her guessing, but kept her life in some sort of balance, as well.

Sitting back beside him in their first criminal law class, Lara pondered his progressive arrival into the center of her world, her judgment less clouded now that she was out of the heat of the moment. She had so many mixed emotions when it came to this man that she couldn't even determine which one was dominant. He was utterly gorgeous—in fact, she still found it hard to think straight in his presence—but he blew hot and cold, and the future was a black hole.

At the end of the day, the question to be asked was whether she was independent and strong enough to be satisfied with only a casual relationship in her life—something she'd never even previously considered. And she realized, with no small amount of relief, that the answer to that question was yes. Lara was sure she had the presence of mind to hold herself together instead of simply pining after Marcus from a distance, and to walk away the minute their arrangement stopped working for her. As long as she kept herself surrounded by razor wire and cyclone fencing, of course.

Self-preservation was the key here. A big part of her already adored him, she knew that. But trust? That was a different matter.

*

On Wednesday, Lara, Marcus, Kate, and Pete gathered for lunch, all finally being free to catch up on each other's holiday news. Pete was considerably less chirpy than usual. He was the only one of them who hadn't attained honors results in his examinable subjects, although he took full responsibility for the underachievement, admitting that he hadn't put in as much effort as was required.

"That's going to have to change now, I suppose," he added reluctantly. "As my dear old dad keeps pointing out, it's time to stop dragging the chain and think longer term. It's a tough call though; Burst has been making a real name for itself, so it's even harder to get excited about conditional contracts or directors' duties than it used to be. And that's saying something…"

"So, all is roses in your boy band now, then? No more lovers' tiffs?" Kate asked teasingly. Pete had told them that there'd been some friction within the band in recent times, as the lead singer Charlie had been less than reliable and committed. Lately, he'd either missed rehearsals altogether or turned up too unfashionably late and wasted to be of much use to the other band members.

"Actually, I would say we're more cacti than roses right now." Pete sighed. "And I don't think it's heading anywhere good in a hurry. Charlie is being a complete tosser, but if I'm really honest, it's *his* looks and stage presence that has got us this far…"

"Do my ears deceive me? Am I really hearing this from Pete 'the sex god' Kingston?" interrupted Kate.

"Hilarious, Katie." Pete stared at her drolly. "It's *not* funny. If it was one of the others behaving like such an idiot, we'd have kicked him out by now. There're plenty of good musicians who could take their places. But Charlie is kind of indispensable as our front man. If he keeps this up though, Burst may very well burst."

"Well, in that case, Pete, your dad's right. Don't give up your day job…"

"I know, I know. My dreams of living in black leather pants, dripping blondes and bling, are being replaced by images of charcoal suits and power ties. It's scary, and really, really sad," Pete replied with a wan smile. "Anyway, in case we die a horrible death in the near future, come and watch us at our big gig in the city next month, will you? I'll put your names on the door. I could really use the support," he added glumly, and the others agreed they would. Pete then turned to Lara, keen to change the subject.

"How about you, girl? Anything interesting to report? And, by that, I mean anything other than the stock standard précis of coastal life?"

Lara glanced meaningfully at Marcus. By unspoken agreement, the pair had kept their holiday encounters from the others, and Lara was not about to open up about them now. So instead, she answered Pete with a description of two of her more hopeful cases at Legal Aid, where she'd spent a couple of days toward the end of the break. One was an immigration matter, while the other involved a young man with a low-level involvement in drug-pushing in Melbourne's outer suburbs. She'd been negotiating hard with the local police to have his charges dropped in exchange for information about the creeps he worked for.

"Good on you, girl," Pete commented approvingly. "Sick the dogs onto the hard core dealers, and get the guy into a community service program. At least then he'll have some slim chance of a decent life. It's the monsters up the totem pole that are really messing everyone up. You should see the state of some of the younger people that come and watch us at night! It's just sick, and getting worse all the time." He shook his head in disgust, while Marcus just watched and listened, thoughtfully.

*

On Friday, the pendulum swung back a bit when Marcus found Lara alone in the library.

"Well, hi there," he whispered into her ear as he slid into the seat next to hers, making her jump.

"Hi yourself," she responded after a moment, when she'd managed to pull her gaze away from his stunning, wind-swept appearance, her pulse racing.

"Am I interrupting?" he asked.

"Yes."

"Oh, sorry…" he replied, but his smirk indicated that he wasn't.

"Don't worry about it." She returned his look knowingly, and the air between them became charged.

"Sooo, I wanted to ask you something," he broke their brief silence with a half-smile, undoubtedly aware of his physical effect on her.

"Okay…?"

"Would you like to go out with me for dinner tomorrow?"

She blinked slowly. "What for?" she couldn't help but ask, and he grinned.

"For the sheer pleasure of my company, Lara. We're going to Pete's gig afterwards anyway…I just thought we could fill in the time beforehand together. What do you think?"

"I think yes," she replied.

"Good. Great. For a minute there, I thought you were going to leave me hanging." An experience he'd most likely never had. "I'll pick you up at six o'clock, okay?"

"I can't wait." She smiled at him.

"Me neither." He dazzled her with a return smile, before leaning down to brush his thumb along her jawline, until it rested momentarily, tantalizingly, at the corner of her mouth. Then, his expression loaded, he stood up without another word and headed off campus to do whatever it was he did. Lara had to laugh at herself, realizing that she couldn't take her eyes off him even as he walked away, captivated by his fluid, almost jaunty stride, suggestive of energy to burn. Where he was off to, she could only guess.

*

Marcus arrived at her door the following evening at the appointed hour, looking as amazing as ever in a finely striped fitted top and dark pants. He simply took her breath away. And he certainly looked fresher than Lara did; she'd tossed and turned all night in anticipation of seeing him alone again, and had faint shadows under her eyes as a result. She just hoped that the tiredness was masked by the light layer of makeup she'd put on after getting changed into her outfit, which consisted of a loose-fitting red top over leggings and boots.

"Hello again, gorgeous!" he greeted her, putting his arms around her and nuzzling into her freshly washed hair. "Mmmm, you look good enough to eat. If I hadn't made a booking, I think I'd have to take you right back inside for some alone time. But the city awaits…"

Lara was mildly disappointed with that decision.

"So, where to?" she asked curiously after she'd grabbed a jacket and they'd walked down the stairs and out to his truck.

"You'll see!" he said with a grin, before pulling out into the traffic and heading south to the other side of the city. He had a Ben Lee CD playing, and Lara hummed along to the familiar music until her favorite track came on and they both sang the chorus at full volume, much to the amusement of the people waiting at the lights in the car next to them. Marcus chuckled and reached out to hold her hand as they cruised along an esplanade in Melbourne's best-known beachside suburb.

"Hungry?" he asked.

"Famished!" Lara said. She'd been too excited to eat much all day…not that she was going to tell him that.

"We're having dinner at the end of St. Kilda pier," he announced as they turned into a car park. "The food's tasty and the servings are huge, which I knew you'd like. I once saw you consume almost a whole loaf of bread in a single sitting, remember?" She punched him on the arm, but smiled happily as they got out of the truck.

"That looks like fun," she said, pointing to some catamarans flying past in a twilight race as they walked along the pier.

"It is." He grinned. Of *course,* he would have tried it. "I crewed for a guy up in Sydney occasionally. Using the wind and the swell together like that, it's wild!"

She couldn't help laughing at his enthusiasm for living.

Once seated, they both ordered a seafood risotto and a white wine. Looking out the floor-to-ceiling windows at the passing parade of sailors, kite surfers, and returning fishermen, and back toward the dog-walkers and cyclists on the boardwalk, Lara commented that she was surprised that there was so much action at a city beach.

"Coming from the coast, I'm embarrassed to admit that I've always snubbed Melbourne's bay beaches. But there's a lot going on here, isn't there? It's fun."

"You should try living in Sydney then," said Marcus. "There's a fantastic scene on the northern beaches, for those who can afford it. People get up for a morning surf or swim before walking home for breakfast, getting into their suits, and jumping on the local ferry to work. Everything's at their fingertips."

"Tell me about growing up there," asked Lara, head in hand, leaning on the table. And, for once, he did. He talked about his love of school and learning, the difficulties of adolescence, his two closest friends, family life both before and after his father had died, and his regular visits back to Sydney to see everyone he cared about. Lara took it all in, fascinated, fitting some more pieces into the puzzle that so intrigued her.

"It sounds idyllic," she said.

"Do you think you'll move back there?" She avoided his gaze, nervous about the response. There was a lengthy pause before he answered.

"I'm not sure. I've always assumed that I would, until recently. Now, well, we'll see."

Lara sighed. There were just so many unanswered questions.

"What about you, anyway?" Marcus asked, changing the subject. "What's the plan after you finish uni? Will you stay in the city, do you think? Not much call for a solicitor in Anglesea, I'm guessing…"

"You've got that right." She smiled. "I'm not quite sure about my plans, either. I'll probably stay here and continue my double life for a few more years. Then, depending on how things are tracking, there's always the possibility of living at the beach and making the commute to Geelong each day. It's not too bad, and there's enough work there for an established solicitor. That's my longer-term goal, I think."

"Nice," Marcus replied, nodding his head in approval. "Sounds like a great balance."

They continued their more serious discussion over coffees and a shared cheese platter. Now that they'd breached the uncomfortable topic of the future, they were keen to keep questioning each other.

"So, apart from living at Anglesea and working as a gun lawyer, what do you think your life will be like in, say, ten years?" Marcus asked curiously. "What will you have done, and what will you be doing?"

Lara wriggled uncomfortably in her chair, unused to sharing her private hopes and dreams with anyone else. Marcus smiled at her obvious discomfort, but sat and waited patiently for her reply. She sighed in resignation.

"Well, I imagine most of my time will be spent keeping the big corporates on their toes," she joked, raising her fist in the air in a half-mocking workers' salute. "But hopefully I'll have notched up a surfing trip to Indonesia, at the very least, and will have my own place. Other than that, I'll just be hanging out beachside with my mates and my mutt, I suppose."

"And?" asked Marcus.

"And what?" Lara responded nervously.

"Any family?" he prompted. She blushed and looked down at her hands before eventually replying.

"I...don't know. It's not something I've ever really thought about. I suppose if I met—and stayed with—the right man, someone who I thought would add to my life and never take from it, then yes, I'd think about marriage, kids, the works. But only then." She took a sip of water and heaved a sigh of relief at having gotten an answer out. Then she looked up at Marcus defiantly. "How about you? Your turn under the microscope."

"Fair enough." He smiled, clearly more comfortable with this discussion than she was. "In ten years, depending on where I am, I'll be working for the Director of Public Prosecutions or even the Australian Crime Commission, I hope, bringing reprobates to justice by the truckload. Idealists, aren't we? Hopefully, I'll have explored some of the lesser-known regions of the world, and done some mountaineering. Everest is even calling my name, I think. And before you ask, despite my wanderlust, I want all the rest as well, Lara: a gorgeous, intelligent wife and heaps of little ankle-biters to greet me when I walk through the front door every evening. Life just wouldn't be complete without family, in my opinion."

She looked at him, speechless, in awe of his self-confidence and the ease with which he spoke of such personal matters. He certainly was an unusual guy. Gran was right; he had the maturity of a significantly older man.

Marcus smiled and reached across to tweak her ear. "Don't look so serious, sunshine…we're supposed to be having fun, remember? Speaking of which, it's probably time we got moving." As it always did when Lara was with him, time had sped by, and the waiting staff had lit the candles at each table in readiness for the later sitting.

"Great," she said, relieved to let her heavier thoughts drift away. Then, despite her protests, he insisted on paying the bill, before stretching as he stood. His top rode up as he did so, revealing a taut stomach that caught and held Lara's gaze.

"Oops, sorry," he said when he realized what he'd done.

"Don't be," she replied, grinning mischievously up at him and giving him a subtle wink.

"Hmm. Now, now…" he warned with a growl, desire flashing fleetingly across his face, only to be quelled at his will. "There'll be none of that nonsense out in public, young lady. Don't lower the tone…"

Lara laughed as she stood to join him, and they wandered slowly back along the pier, stopping to investigate the fishermen's catches and amble through a street market along the way. Then, when they got back to the boardwalk, Marcus stopped and gave her a spontaneous hug under one of the streetlights.

"This is awesome, Lara. I can't get over how much fun I have just hanging out with you. Do you feel that too?"

"I don't want today to end," she replied simply, as they broke apart and continued to the parking lot. Being around him had been electrifying from the first moment she'd laid eyes on him. But now, with the passage of time and the clearing of hurdles, there was a layer of comfort in addition to the excitement, and it felt even better than she could ever have imagined.

"Although, I kind of wish we didn't have a gig to go to right now," Lara admitted as they reached the truck, leaning against it as she waited for him to get his keys out. "It's not really what I'm in the mood for anymore."

"I know what you mean. But we've got to go and fly the flag, for Pete's sake. If you'll pardon the pun. And we'll be there together, don't forget…" He leaned his body into hers against the truck rather than unlocking it, making the hairs stand up on the back of her neck. "Which isn't all bad, is it?" he whispered into her ear, before trailing his lips lower and kissing her so sensually down her jaw and neck that she thought her heart might leap out of her ribcage. For a full minute, she couldn't think straight, or even breathe.

Then, though, he pulled his head back with a reluctant sigh, and after a soft, sweet kiss on the lips, he gathered her in his arms and they stood entwined, sharing time and space for a precious minute. Gazing up at the twinkling lights of the city over his shoulder, Lara relived their evening together and smiled. She told herself that, somehow, they were a step closer to climbing out of no-man's-land and onto solid ground.

How wrong she was, and how quickly her world was about to come tumbling down.

Chapter 18

Lara and Marcus walked down the stairs of the appointed city bar together only a short time later, laughing about what a far cry it was from the warm, inviting restaurant they'd just left. They immediately got talking to different people, however, and she barely laid eyes on him for the rest of the night in the crowded, dimly lit venue. But Lara didn't mind. Burst was as fired up as ever, and she sat and enjoyed singing along to some of the now-familiar numbers while chatting easily with Kate. Without making a conscious decision, she kept the news of her date with Marcus to herself once again, preferring to reflect over it later, in private.

As she sat, she recalled what Pete had told them about Charlie's erratic behavior. She watched the lead singer more closely, and noticed that he seemed quite unaware of his surroundings and out of sync with what the rest of the band were doing. He was off on some tangent of his own, strutting and preening as he went. While his almost feline sensuality on stage was undeniable, it was a testament to the talent of the rest of the band members that they managed to adapt to his rapid shifts in focus, and produce a cohesive sound. Lara caught a particularly frustrated look between the Jackson brothers as Charlie stopped one of their most popular tunes mid-chorus to rip off his shirt and jump down to dance with some of his ever-eager female groupies.

"Who does he think he is, Mick Jagger?" asked Kate, a disgusted look on her face. "What an idiot! Poor Pete."

Pete came and joined his friends at the end of the set, his agitation more than apparent. Lara bought him a beer, and his friends tried to soothe him with their praise, but he was painfully aware of the reality of the situation.

"Thanks, guys, you're the best, and I'm really grateful for your support. But, the writing's on the wall, and we all know it. Ted and Tony and I thought we'd just see how tonight went, and whether, by some miracle, Charlie might settle down when it really mattered. But he is who he is, and we've now got a big decision to make about the band's future." Pete shrugged as he took a swig of his drink, not one to harbor false illusions. "Don't feel you have to stay all the way through, by the way. In my experience, things are only going to go downhill from here."

Lara was grateful for the out Pete provided. Her sleepless night was starting to catch up with her, and that fatigue, combined with the fact that she'd just seen a cockroach run across their table, made her want to get out of the grungy, underground cavern, and seek the solace of her cozy flat. And so, making her goodbyes, she looked around the room to find Marcus, to no avail. Eventually, disappointed at such an anticlimactic end to their evening together, she asked Kate to pass on her "good night," and tell him that she'd talk to him soon.

With a final wave, she walked up the stairs of the club and out into the dark of the city night. Zipping up her jacket in preparation for the walk home, Lara went to cross the street, passing between two parked cars as she went. As she did so though, her attention was caught by a movement in the second car, and she automatically looked closer. Then she stopped in her tracks. Despite the fact that his back was partially turned and he was in animated conversation with the other occupant, she was sure it was Marcus. Without thinking about it further, Lara leaned across and rapped smartly on the window, smiling with relief at having found him. But her smile slowly fell away as Marcus whipped around with a look of alarm that remained even once he'd recognized her. And then Lara saw the reason for his discomfort—the other occupant. The redhead.

Marcus hurriedly opened his door and got out, while the girl climbed more slowly from the driver's side. She was dressed in a low-cut top, mini-skirt, and boots, and looked sensational. Lara was speechless, more because of the expression on Marcus's face than the situation itself.

"Aahh, Lara, this is Tory…Victoria," he finally said, filling the awkward silence that ensued.

"Nice to meet you," Tory said with the shadow of a smile as she leaned against the car. "I've seen you at these gigs, but we've never formally met."

"Right. Hi," Lara replied weakly, before turning her gaze back to Marcus. "I didn't realize you two knew each other."

"We don't!" Tory quickly jumped in. "That is, we didn't until tonight. Then we got talking about music, and decided to come out here where we could hear ourselves think."

"Is that right?" Lara enquired, the question for Marcus alone.

"Yeah, it is," he confirmed in a strained voice, after a long pause. His expression was now awash with guilt.

"You wanted some privacy, so you could talk—about music," Lara sought confirmation.

"Well, we got chatting about other stuff too," Tory said brightly. "The time got away from us a bit. In fact, we should all probably head back inside now to catch the second set, don't you think? The boys won't be too happy if all of their mates abandon them in their hour of need!" She looked at her watch and stifled a yawn, then leaned in to lock up the car.

"We'll catch you up, Tory," Marcus said to her, his eyes never leaving Lara's. Tory shrugged nonchalantly and raised her hand in a brief wave as she turned and headed back into the club. Lara was confused; the girl hadn't shown overt signs of possessiveness or even attraction toward Marcus, and yet his own shameful face told a completely different story.

"A strange end to an intense evening, then," Lara said to him softly, once they were alone. "Not one I'd expected."

"No, I know. I'm sorry, I wasn't thinking. We really were just talking music…Tory knows a stack about it, and I didn't come out here for any other reason…" He took up her limp hand and held it tightly.

But his explanation was weak, and her internal alarm was stronger. Stunning guy, sexy girl, alone in the night. What else could it all mean? Lara drew a blank; there were just no other feasible explanations. And she realized that, almost regardless of what had or hadn't transpired between Marcus and Tory tonight, the insecurity itself was unbearably painful. So this was the flipside of falling for someone so gorgeous—a life accompanied by the fear of loss.

Which was no longer acceptable.

Because if there was one thing that Lara knew about herself, it was that she wasn't going to live like that again…she'd already lost enough. Her mind was screaming, and there was a stabbing sensation in her chest, but she knew instinctively what had to be done. Act now, immediately, and deal with the pain later, she directed herself robotically. And so, extricating her hand carefully from his and taking a deep breath, Lara reached into her reserves of strength and resilience to impart her message with force.

"Marcus, it's okay; no further explanation needed. I get it. This is the age-old guy/girl impasse, isn't it? We've just arrived here really quickly…" She held up her hand and smiled sadly as he tried to speak. "No, let me finish, please. You've sought out another woman's company this evening, for whatever reason, after the incredibly nice dinner we had. And that's obviously fine with you, despite the 'one-woman guy' routine. But it's not fine with me. I've been happy enough to go along with a less than binding commitment—even though it's far from my ideal—but I draw the line when other people become involved, I'm afraid."

"Please, Lara, it's not what you think…"

"Then what is it, Marcus?" her voice rang out with barely concealed emotion. "Tell me how else to interpret your sitting out here for almost an hour with a beautiful woman, while the rest of us are inside? If you've got a good explanation, I'd really love to hear it!" But at that challenge, Marcus just looked back at her helplessly, unable to provide her with a convincing answer.

"I didn't think so," she said more quietly, and it could have been a stranger's voice. "Listen, it's been a great ride, while it's lasted, and I'll always treasure it. I think we've gotten to know each other pretty well, and you've said some lovely things that I'm sure you meant, at the time. I know you're not a complete phony! But it ends now. We're too different, and I don't want a rocky road, I just don't. You've been keeping your distance all along, really, so I'm sure you can understand. I should have listened to the warning bells sooner, but I get the message now. All right?"

The words thankfully out, Lara watched carefully to see if her point had hit home. For a minute, Marcus just stared back at her, the strain apparent in his features. Eventually though, he closed his eyes before exhaling deeply and shaking his head.

"I *knew* this would happen. My fault, my loss." He seemed to be talking to himself more than to Lara. Then he surprised her by taking both of her hands in his and moving closer, speaking desperately with his face only inches from hers.

"Lara, I understand why you're saying these things, believe me. I'd probably react exactly the same way in your position. But, listen to me—I beg you! Don't write me off just yet, okay? I think things might be able to be different—better—for us. Maybe not today, but soon. Please…?" His beautiful blue eyes were piercing into her soul.

As always, when confronted with Marcus's physical presence, Lara found his entreaty difficult to resist. She recalled all of his recent endearments and tender admissions with yearning, wanting more than anything to believe in their time together. If only things between them could be completely right! But her independence and self-worth were at stake, and she couldn't allow him to keep stringing her along; she just couldn't. And that instinct for self-preservation helped to keep her resolute, even as she felt her dreams disintegrating around her.

"No." She shook her head firmly. "We are who we are, Marcus. This is the end of the line for me, and I'm not going back."

A shocked silence, before he made his final plea.

"Believe in me," he whispered, his voice raw with emotion and his face ashen.

Lara stared at him, a sinking feeling in the pit of her stomach. That was the issue at the very core of everything, after all. Could she trust him? With an aching heart, she knew the answer. Already, she could feel the numbness spreading inside her, her body's natural protection against the impending pain.

"I can't," she finally whispered back, looking down at the ground in front of her, starting to feel choked up with the intensity of her own distress. "I have to go," was all she could say, pulling her hands roughly out of his and stepping backwards. Then, before the telltale tears could cloud her eyes, she turned abruptly and headed for home, without once looking back.

*

Not much later that night, Lara tucked herself into bed and curled up in the fetal position, finally allowing the pain to flood through her body. She felt sick to her stomach about the downward spiral of the night. Such was the nature of life and caring for other people, she tried to console herself…you just never knew when things were suddenly going to blow up in your face. There was no doubt that Marcus was an incredible man, and her feelings for him were electric. But she was only half surprised that they'd crashed and burned so quickly, after the pleasure-pain of the last three months. In the end, her head had overruled her heart, and that's just the way it was meant to be.

Tossing and turning for the next couple of hours while trying to keep the threatening tears at bay, Lara finally fell into an exhausted sleep. But her dreams were bad ones, and she woke early the next morning with a sense of dread before she'd even fully remembered the previous night's events. Then, when even a strong cup of coffee failed to work its magic, she decided to write off the day, and merely to bunker down in her apartment with a good book and some comfort food. And there she stayed, holed up for the remainder of the day, steeling herself to re-enter the real world as soon as she could face it.

*

As it turned out, finding some sort of normality back at uni wasn't as hard as Lara had feared it would be. Marcus was often absent from classes, and even when he was there, he kept to the fringes around her, rather than seeking out her company. Which suited her fine. During the few times when they sat in the same group in the cafeteria, he was courteous but subdued, giving her no more or less attention than he would a casual acquaintance.

It was as if Marcus too wished to banish their brief history from his mind, for his own reasons. And because he didn't make a big deal out of the heady times they'd shared, Lara was able to ignore them as well. Their close encounters drifted off into a distant dreamland in her mind. In her state of denial, their connection might've been something that had happened to someone else, long ago.

Now that her social life had apparently fallen to pieces, she was more determined than ever to put her head down and finish the academic year somewhere near the top. And that meant submitting some standout essays over the next month and being totally prepared for exam time, come November.

In the library, she went about collecting the various reports she needed to prepare detailed plans for her two biggest papers. She plowed through the heavy volumes for hours, making the occasional notation on her pad when further references of interest were mentioned. In particular, an idea started to form in relation to her torts assignment…she decided to use her father's accident as a case study in the fields of negligence and manufacturers' liability. She wanted to determine whether, with access to the right legal practitioner and resources, they could have won his case.

*

As a distraction from her woes, Lara even accepted a dinner date with Will Lancaster from the law ball, after bumping into him out the front of the library. They went out to a local French restaurant, and talked easily about the university experience and what they did in their civilian lives.

His company was entertaining, and the conversation flowed with lots of easy laughs. She felt strangely at ease with Will's transparent flirting—a part of her responded to his relaxed manner and his "easy come, easy go" mentality. And she knew she could do a lot worse than spending an evening with this handsome, uncomplicated guy. But as the evening wore on and they walked up the eclectic Italian shopping strip near the uni for Melbourne's best gelati, Lara acknowledged to herself that something was missing. Will was a nice guy, but there was no real spark.

So when the date eventually culminated at her front door, she gave him a quick kiss on the cheek and stood back, communicating silently that she was calling it a night. With an understanding grin, Will told her in his comfortable way that he'd had fun, and was available for another date any time she felt like one. And that was that.

Chapter 19

It was only a couple of weeks later that the next bombshell exploded.

It was a Wednesday morning, and Lara had made her now-standard trio of coffees and knocked on Daniel's door for breakfast. This morning, it was Dan who opened up, resplendent as ever in his designer suit as he tied his brightly colored tie. But the look on his face was guarded.

"Ahh, hi, Lara. Come on in, we were just talking about you."

"You were? How come?"

"I'll let Daniel explain, honey. I've got to get into work early." Dan leaned forward and gave her a kiss, taking a couple of gulps of the proffered coffee before calling out to Daniel and departing the scene. Lara waited expectantly on a stool at the kitchen bench until Daniel emerged from the bathroom, enveloped in a cloud of aftershave.

"So, what's up?" Lara enquired of him. "Dan said you'd been talking about me? Must have been fascinating..."

"Well, it was, actually, princess," said Daniel. "Surprisingly." As she raised her eyebrow sardonically, her friend picked up a folded newspaper, and presented it to her with a dramatic bow. Lara absorbed the highlighted headline grudgingly, before sitting up straighter and paying more attention.

Burst Busted
Sex, drugs, and rock 'n' roll!
A carefully coordinated police operation ended last night with raids on three houses belonging to musicians from local rock band Burst. Police sources have confirmed that one of

the premises contained trafficable quantities of amphetamines and barbiturates, and that the lead singer, Charlie Davis, has been charged with seven drug-related offences, while the other band members are still being held for questioning. The illicit substances were allegedly being sold at the band's performances in various live music venues throughout Melbourne, concealed within merchandise items. One follower of the band commented that it was well known in the live music scene that Mr. Davis had high-level contacts in Melbourne's underworld. The matter is listed to appear before the Magistrates' Court next month.

Lara scanned the article twice, before looking up at Daniel, pale with shock.

"Oh my God, Daniel!"

"I know, it sucks. Poor Pete..."

"I just can't believe this. It sounds like he's in police custody! But there's no way he was involved in any of this...*none*. I know him better than that. He's got a lot of time for beer, but none for drugs. Where would he be?"

"Fitzroy station would be my bet."

"Right. Thanks. I'd better see what I can do." With a promise to keep him informed, she ran back into her flat to turn on her phone with shaking hands, breakfast forgotten. Thankfully, she got through to Kate on the third ring.

"Thank God, Lara!"

"Kate! What the hell's going on?"

"I've already made a few calls. Apparently Pete's still being questioned in Fitzroy about any potential involvement in this mess. He's been there for half the night, with Ted and Tony. I just can't believe it's happening. It's absurd! I've never heard Pete say a single damned thing linking him to drugs, have you? It just doesn't sound right."

"No way, not with his social conscience. As for Charlie,

though…well, nothing that guy got involved in would surprise me. But Pete's totally different."

"Agreed. And God knows what this is going to do to his legal career. I still feel like I'm dreaming. This is way out of my comfort zone. But, I know that Pete's going to need our support, Lara. I'm off to the station now to see if there's anything that can be done from our end…"

"Right behind you. I'll meet you there in half an hour," replied Lara.

As it happened, their timing was perfect. The two girls were in the middle of harassing the desk sergeant when notification came through that Pete was about to be released. Ten minutes later, he appeared through a security door, and the girls flung their arms around him immediately. Dressed in his clothes from the night before, he looked tired and haggard, but his trademark lopsided grin still managed to find its way onto his face.

"Sorry to put you out, ladies. But nice to see your friendly faces. Just hang ten while I jump through a couple more hoops, will you? They've still got my things. Then I could really use a decent breakfast!"

Lara and Kate went back out onto the street to wait for Pete's processing to be finalized. When Kate went around the corner to get her car, though, Lara looked up and swore she saw a familiar figure walking up some nearby steps to enter into the police station through a separate side entrance.

"Marcus?" she called tentatively, but the man kept walking and disappeared through the door. She must've been mistaken, Lara realized. The stranger had been dressed in a jacket and cap in the cool of the morning, so it could have been anyone. She was obviously still overly fixated on Marcus, despite her best efforts to move forward.

Pete eventually emerged, to be greeted by a group cheer and more hugs all round, as well as a good-natured declaration from

Kate that he looked like hell and smelled like ex-con trash. The threesome then piled into Kate's car and drove to a well-frequented café nearby to order plates loaded with bacon and eggs and mega coffees, before quieting down to hear Pete's sorry story.

In short, the police had detained him during a shift at the pub the previous evening, as part of a series of raids around Melbourne. They'd already searched his house and talked to his two flat-mates, before taking him to the station for questioning. There, he was locked up for a couple of hours, presumably while the police collated their findings. Then, although treating him well and following necessary procedure, they'd gone over and over the same questions for hours at various intervals during the night, obviously trying to trip him up if there were any holes in his story. He'd rejected the offer of representation, much to Kate's disgust, as he'd had absolutely nothing to hide. He'd known none of the people whose photos were pushed in front of him time and again, although recognized a couple of faces from the audience at Burst gigs. He hadn't known that Charlie had been dealing drugs, although admitted knowing that he was a serious user and that he'd had numerous fights with him in recent times about how it was affecting the band. The police must have finally believed him to be innocent, given his release, and he was convinced the Jackson brothers would be discharged shortly too.

"And so," he finished in his understated, resilient manner as the breakfast plates arrived and were ravenously attacked, "here I am, slightly on the nose—as you so kindly pointed out, Katie—but living to tell the tale."

"Is the end of your involvement in the matter, then?" Lara asked, uncertain of the particulars of the process.

"Well, the cops told me to be prepared for more questioning, but I doubt it'll be necessary. I've already told them all I know, repeatedly. So, apart from having to cancel bookings and other commitments of the band, there's nothing more to it. The best thing we can do is just to put it all behind us as quickly as possible and get back to normal. Well, except for one thing, that is. About Marcus, I'm afraid."

Kate looked at him quizzically, while Lara went cold.

"He's been here with me all night," Pete continued.

"What? They were questioning him too?" Lara asked, confused.

"No..."

"You mean you called *him*, rather than us?" Kate interrupted incredulously.

"No, I didn't." Pete shook his head slowly. "He's a cop, guys. An undercover cop."

Lara just stared at him, unable to move a muscle.

"*What?*" cried Kate.

"He came and told me when I was locked up, then stayed with me the entire time I was questioned. I know, I know..." he said in response to his friends' stunned looks. "I can hardly believe it either, and I've had hours to digest the news. I'm still not sure how I feel about it all. There were three of them tagging on our case over the last three months, apparently, working as part of a bigger team that covered other higher-level connections. That cute redheaded girl who was hanging out with Ted and Tony, she was one of them. And some other guy who was always in a black leather jacket, ostensibly buying from Charlie. They wore wires in the end, which is how they gathered enough evidence to arrest him."

"So all this time, he's just been planted at uni to get close to you guys...he's not a real law student at all," Kate mused, voicing her wonderment out loud. "My God, the lengths they've gone to! He's so established there, it's like he's part of the furniture...what a brilliant cover!" Then, after a nudge from Pete, she looked across at Lara's white face.

"Oh, Lar, I'm sorry! I don't mean to sound admiring, I'm not condoning his behavior or anything. His job obviously involves living a lie, and we've all been caught up in it. And as for his flirting with you, that totally sucks. I'm just amazed that he was able to fool everyone so easily. Now that I think about it, though, he's always seemed a lot older than the rest of us. Who knows what his real life's like?"

Lara was barely registering what Kate was saying, her mind reeling in shock at Pete's news. But with Kate's final comments, she rose abruptly and fled to the empty bathroom, hearing Pete's quiet but acerbic "Way to throw salt on a wound, Katie" as the door slammed shut behind her. Leaning on one of the cold ceramic sinks with two shaking hands, she forced herself to focus on preventing the threatened anxiety attack, taking slow, deliberate breaths with her eyes closed. Then, her heart still slamming in her chest, she sank down onto the floor and leant her head on the wall behind her, trying to relax all of her clenched muscles and take control of her panic. Marcus…an undercover agent.

Who'd only pursued her to get closer to Pete, and to get the answers he was looking for in his job.

A complete stranger who'd lied to her over and over again, until she'd fallen for him.

And, worst of all, who'd been in her homes, and even charmed her grandmother, for Christ's sake!

How low could a person go? Lara shook her head, unable to absorb the enormity of the façade. She felt frozen in time, unable to move, and was unsure how long she sat there, staring at nothing.

Eventually, Kate peered tentatively through the door. "Lara, honey, are you okay in here?" Her voice mirrored the concern on her face.

"No."

"Then why don't you come on out and talk about it with us?"

"Just give me another minute," Lara replied blankly, before standing once more and looking at her strained appearance in the mirror. She ran the cold tap and rubbed handfuls of water over her face, trying without much luck to wash away the self-pity and dismay. Finally, she toweled herself off before taking a deep breath and walking back out to her friends. Their faces looked up at hers with sadness, empathy, and warmth. They had suffered a betrayal as well, and they understood her pain. She could rely on their support, just as Pete had been able to rely on hers.

"Sorry, guys. I just can't believe…" she began, before the tears welled unexpectedly in her eyes. Then the other two were both leaning toward her with hugs and helping to drive away the despair. In a choked voice, she told them what had happened over the last few weeks, and about some of the things that Marcus had said about his feelings, seemingly as besotted with their relationship as she had been. Kate was outraged.

"How dare he? How *dare* he?" she kept repeating, before sitting back in a slump and suggesting that they try to get Marcus suspended from the force for becoming personally involved with someone related to his case, while Pete offered to give him a few hard kicks in the groin if they ever laid eyes on him again. Unbelievably, at that last suggestion, a weak laugh bubbled up from Lara's throat.

"What would I do without you guys?" She smiled weakly at her friends through puffy eyes. "I suppose I'll get over this, just as you will, Pete. But what on earth did we do to deserve this?"

"Nothing." Pete shrugged. "Stuff happens. Then you die."

"Oh, that explains everything…what an awesome philosophy, Pete!" Kate responded sarcastically. "When you *do* die, I'm going to organize to have that written on your headstone. It really sums up the complex kind of guy you are…"

And, amazingly, with their standard banter and some more hugs and handholding, the drama became manageable.

*

That night, Lara put Powderfinger on the stereo, opened some red wine, and drank too much of it. Although some raw memories continued to flash through her brain, the protective effects of shock continued to shelter her from the enormity of what she'd learnt, and she remained mostly numb. At some point during the evening, Daniel banged on the door to join her after work. He helped himself to a wine glass from the kitchen and filled it up, before turning down the stereo and taking a seat on her couch, where she joined him.

"Okay. Tell me everything," he instructed her.

Taking a deep breath, she told him all about what had happened to Pete, before sharing the revelation about Marcus's real job. Daniel listened in silence, awestruck. When she'd finally finished, he gave a long, low whistle.

"Phew, girl, you *have* been worked over! No wonder you look like such a wreck…" Her eyes narrowed and she gave him a "thanks for nothing" look. "Sorry. I'm just stunned that you've been caught up in all this excitement. You're usually so…*conservative*, if you don't mind my saying so, and this is real tabloid trash."

"Tell me about it. I'm still in complete shock. For a while there, I thought I might have been entering a serious relationship, even though there were clearly issues beneath the surface. But now I find out that every minute I spent with Marcus was a lie."

"Maybe not…" Daniel stared into his wine glass thoughtfully.

"What do you mean?"

"Well, let's review all of the facts, Sherlock. One: Marcus seems like a great guy, and I'm not easily fooled. Two: Think about the way he looks at you! I don't reckon you can fake that, especially for so long. And three: Getting involved with you might've actually made things harder for him on the job, not easier. He didn't need to do that to get friendly with Pete. Have you even considered that maybe his feelings for you are real? That he just couldn't help himself? You can't choose who you fall in love with, after all. And an undercover cop…I mean, personally, I think that's hot!"

Lara stared at her friend incredulously. Marcus's deception was many things, but she'd hardly describe it as "hot."

"How…how can you say that?" she managed to splutter. "He's completely used me to get what he wanted, Daniel. I would have thought you'd be on my side all the way on this…"

"I am, honey, I am." He sighed, leaning across to hold her warmly. "Okay then, the bloke is a total snake! Seriously, though, I'm just trying to point out that it might not be as bad as you think. I reckon you should at least give him a hearing, assuming he contacts you. Which he will. You never know where that conversation might lead. I think it'd be worth it; good guys are extremely hard to find, as we both know. And if nothing else, it'll give you proper closure."

"No way," she blurted out. "I have absolutely no interest in talking to that phony ever again. I've been duped long enough, Daniel. It's over."

"Fair enough." He held up his hands in surrender. "Your call, obviously. I'm just so sorry you've been put through all of this, Lara. It's been so good to see you happy. We need to keep this momentum going. I'm going to focus my energies on finding you a *real* Romeo now."

"Don't even think about it." She finally smiled. "I've had enough excitement in the relationship department to last me the next few years. Or maybe forever. It's back to the quiet life for this lone wolf."

Chapter 20

The next day dawned, crisp and clear. Unlike Lara's brain.

Groaning through the fog of a hangover, she stumbled into the kitchen to down a couple of glasses of water before turning on the coffee machine. As she went through the motions of her morning routine, she made a snap decision to give university a miss for the rest of the week. She packed a bag and made her way to the train station, drawn to the haven Anglesea provided. When her train arrived noisily at the platform, she climbed aboard like a zombie and found a window seat. She sat motionless for the hour-long trip, staring out the window at nothing, re-absorbing the impact of the revelation about Marcus and berating herself for her stupidity. Bit by bit, her sluggish mind managed to fit the pieces of the jigsaw together, until she was able to see how totally she'd been played.

Walking up the path to Gran's house later that morning, Lara was still dazed and lifeless. Chief must have sensed her mood, because instead of his usual boisterous greeting, he stood watching her approach from the front door, whining quietly. Gran was summoned by such unusual behavior and came out as well.

"What is it, love?" she asked nervously, as Lara stopped just in front of her.

"It's Marcus, Gran. It was all a complete lie…he's a cop, for God's sake, an undercover cop! He arrested Pete; can you believe it?" The words came tumbling out. Hearing herself say them aloud seemed to open the floodgates, and she finally fell apart. She'd made it home, but didn't have an ounce of energy left to move on from there.

Dropping her bag on the ground and flinging herself into the comfort of her grandmother's arms, she started to sob, great heaving sounds that racked through her entire body. Gran listened to Lara's words with obvious dismay, before allowing her granddaughter to lean on her while she cried the violent tears that so desperately needed to surface. Then, when the sobbing had abated a little, the older woman patted Lara on the back and took her on the first small steps down the long road to recovery.

"Shhh, come on, darling. Come inside. Oh, it sounds like you've been through quite an ordeal, but it's all going to be all right. You're here now, and Chief and I are going to take good care of you. Everything will be as right as rain, you'll see."

Lara stayed in bed for two days. She was strung out and exhausted, but only slept fitfully between bouts of lying there and staring at the ceiling, thinking about everything and nothing. Gran made her soup and chocolate chip biscuits. Chief spent most of his time lying next to her bed, occasionally standing up and wagging, begging unsuccessfully to be taken for a walk.

By Saturday however, Gran had obviously decided that Lara had wallowed for long enough. Walking into her granddaughter's stale bedroom at nine o'clock in the morning, she opened up the blinds and addressed the dopey, blinking girl.

"Right. Time to get up now, missy. Tea and toast are waiting for you in the kitchen, and then I'd like you to shower and join me in the garden. There's work to be done, and you're no use to me moping about in here. I know that that boy has broken your heart, but the girl lying here in utter defeat is not the girl her father raised her to be, God rest his soul. What do you think he'd say if he were here? He'd tell you to get up and at 'em, wouldn't he? And so you will. Up!" Then she marched out of the room, banging around in the kitchen to make sure Lara got the message.

Gran's cajoling worked. As soon as Lara went outside, she knew it was time to get over herself. She walked straight across to her grandmother and gave her the bear hug she'd always loved, and they laughed weakly together. Working side by side, the two women chatted away about more normal matters, and the world around Lara slowly began to take shape again.

The next morning, Lara rose at dawn and walked over the sand dunes in her wetsuit, board under her arm. She stood at the top of the rise and gazed across the vast expanse of water in front of her, glimmering golden in the sunrise, calm today except for the rolling surf. It was more peaceful and more beautiful than any photograph or painting could ever capture, and this morning it was hers alone. Lara was suddenly hit with a good dose of perspective, a lesson the endless ocean often taught her. All of her grieving and pining for a mere mortal meant absolutely nothing in the scheme of things. The world would keep turning and the seasons would change whether she was happy or sad, in Melbourne or in Anglesea, attached or single. At the end of the day, she was part of something bigger, better, more beautiful than her thoughts and worries.

And it felt good to remember that.

*

The following week saw Lara back at university, back in the swing. It seemed that everything there had kicked off again very normally, once the small stir created by Pete's ordeal had blown over. Most of his fellow students had had no idea that he was in a band, let alone its name, and so remained oblivious to what had transpired. But the more social group was better informed, and did their fair share of whispering and pointing across the lecture theatres. A couple of guys actually approached him directly to ask about what had happened, but Pete brushed them off, just repeating that the drama had nothing to do with him and he didn't yet know about the band's future.

There was no sign of Marcus, of course, and it seemed that nobody was aware of his covert involvement in the operation.

In fact, Lara had just made it through Tuesday's criminal law class, confronted by countless unnerving memories, when Sally approached and asked whether she knew the reason for his continued absence. Lara merely shook her head and shrugged before walking away. What a different couple of months they had ahead of them.

After her last lecture finished that Friday, Lara took a run around the university track. She was just completing the final lap when she noticed Marcus's achingly familiar figure watching her from the sidelines. He was standing and leaning against the wall of the adjoining sports complex, dressed in a black polo neck jumper and jeans, handsome beyond belief. Slowing to a walk, Lara made her way to her discarded gym bag without looking at him, swallowed some water, and toweled her face dry. Then, picking up her belongings, she turned and walked slowly and deliberately over to where he stood. Despite herself, she felt her heart start to race, and had to take some discrete deep breaths before the inevitable confrontation.

He straightened up as she approached, and she noticed that his face looked as tired and drawn as her own had all week. Good. They just stood and stared at each other in a Mexican standoff, both guarded, until Lara cleared her throat, ready to speak her mind.

"What the hell are you doing here?" she almost snarled, and saw his eyes widen at the aggression in her voice.

"I came to see you."

Lara didn't miss a beat. "Well, I'm sorry that you've wasted a trip back to this *student* campus, but I have absolutely no interest in talking to you, Marcus."

"Fair enough," he said slowly in his gravelly voice, and she saw regret in his eyes. "But I thought if I came to you, you might be kind enough to give *me* a brief hearing."

"Well, you thought wrong."

"Please, Lara! Just give me five minutes to explain some things…"

"No! Why on earth should I?" Her voice rose with emotion.

"Because surely there's enough history between us that you owe me the chance to…"

"I don't owe you a single damned thing!" she yelled at him furiously, her whole body tensing as the hurt and rejection resurfaced. "You've messed with my head enough! Go and pretend to make friends with someone else, because I'm not in the least bit interested."

If he was shocked by the ferocity of her outburst, he didn't show it, merely looking at her with a concerned and frustrated frown. "Lara, I understand why you're so angry. But I wish you'd hear me out…"

"Well, bad luck! There's nothing you could possibly say to me that I want to hear. I really couldn't care less about how you feel. And FYI, I feel *absolutely nothing* for you, do you hear me? Nothing. So just go back to whatever shadowy life it is that you lead, and leave me alone. You make me sick."

At her last, forceful comment, a look of immense sadness washed across Marcus's face. Lara felt a momentary pinprick of guilt at the harshness of her words, before making a conscious effort to stifle it.

"Then it really is all over," he said quietly, after a moment's pause. "I wish it hadn't come to this, Lara. But I suppose it's only fair that you call the shots now. So, it's goodbye, I guess." He swallowed as he spoke these last words. "And good luck. I'm just so, so sorry for everything."

"Not half as sorry as I am," she replied dismissively, before turning swiftly back toward the campus without so much as a backwards glance.

*

Aside from that unfortunate meeting, however, the faculty simply moved forward without its most controversial student, a little less interesting and colorful for his disappearance. And Lara was surprised to realize that, as the weeks passed and time worked its magic, even her own thoughts of Marcus gradually receded. For the most part.

As the business end of the semester arrived in earnest, the workload increased accordingly. Lara, Kate, and now even Pete attacked the work with vigor, forming a new study group for contracts and torts, to help make the overwhelming amount of review and research more manageable. For the hundredth time that year, Lara thanked her lucky stars for her friends. Their bond had transformed her whole university experience from a solitary, daunting one into a pleasant feeling of belonging and connectedness, and she was confident that they'd keep in touch for life, no matter where their career paths took them.

Assignments were finally submitted, and marks came back a week later. Lara did well in her subjects, and none more so than torts, where she received first class honors for her highly personal case study. With the mixed emotions of a vested interest, she rang Gran to report back. They both felt the same: proud of Lara's efforts, but ultimately convinced and saddened that not enough had been done for her father's cause. Lara felt something else too—an affirmation of her choice of career and a renewed confidence in her abilities in the field.

Finally, exam week came around. Arriving early for her criminal law exam on Thursday, she was at the head of the queue walking in, and was seated right near the front of the room, where she remained happily undistracted by the movement and noises behind her. At the "Pens down!" announcement three hours later, she sat back and stretched, before massaging her aching right hand. Inside, though, she felt relieved, having worked her way comfortably through yet another paper. She was starting to see the light at the end of what had been an extremely long tunnel, and could almost smell the sea air waiting ahead of her.

Walking out of the hall in that dreamy state, she was completely unprepared for the surprise ahead. Amid the audible relief and debriefing taking place amongst the crowd, one small group of students was more animated than the others. Looking up, Lara saw that it was Sally and Kristen, and that they were talking to none other than Marcus Black.

Chapter 21

Standing stock still in amazement, Lara could now decipher their excited exclamations and questions upon seeing him again. What was he doing here? They thought he'd dropped out of the course? How could he sit the crim exam when he'd missed nearly two months' of classes?

Fending off their curiosity and interest with quiet, brief answers, Marcus then stopped answering them completely when his searching gaze located Lara only a few meters away. Their gazes locked and the two stood staring, oblivious to the noise and movement around them. The other girls eventually walked off to join the tail end of students departing the scene, a complaint of "rude behavior" filtering into Lara's consciousness from a long way away. But mostly, she was just adjusting to seeing that striking face again, out of place amid the otherwise muted, bland backdrop. Dressed in his trademark fitted t-shirt and old jeans but with his hair cropped more closely than before, he looked thinner than he had previously, his expression more drawn. Probably working on a stressful case, she supposed. But still the most perfect looking person she'd ever laid eyes on.

Breaking the mutual assessment, Marcus took a couple of steps forward, clearly apprehensive about the waiting reception.

"Hi," he greeted her softly.

"Hi yourself."

"Long time, no see."

"I thought it would be longer. What are you doing here?"

"I'm still enrolled. I told you the truth when I said I wanted to be a prosecutor. I've just been studying online and on my own time outside of work," he explained. "I thought that would be—easier."

"I see," she said slowly, absorbing the unexpected news. "I didn't see you at the other exams?"

"You were focused on the job at hand. I saw you, though."

"Oh." She wondered why none of her friends had mentioned the huge news of his re-appearance, but then remembered that she'd avoided them and her phone all week. Chances were there'd be a couple of incredulous text messages waiting for her, unread.

"You look well, Lara."

"You look tired, Marcus." But as unbelievably gorgeous as ever.

"Well, it's been hard trying to balance full-time work and study…I didn't drop any of the subjects, given how far I'd come with them. But the exam preparation has been much more challenging than I thought it would be. I'll definitely be doing things differently next year."

Next year. Christ almighty.

"Hmm. Right. Well, if you'll excuse me…I've still got one more exam tomorrow…" she started to say while repositioning her bag higher onto her shoulder, eager to get away from the weird scene and process all of this new information. She couldn't even begin to work out how she was feeling about seeing him again.

"Lara, wait!" He reached out and gently held onto her forearm, causing her to take a sharp intake of breath. "We're here together now. Can we please talk, just quickly? I know you absolutely hate my guts, and I accept that. But I really want to explain a couple of things, and try to clear the air between us, to the extent that I can." He paused, and then jumped in again, sensing her uncertainty. "Oh, come on! They say closure is an important step in healing, don't they? I'll do the talking; you don't have to say anything. And I'll be brief, I promise."

Lara was torn. A big part of her wanted to escape and avoid an uncomfortable trip down memory lane. But looking at his pleading face, she also acknowledged that she retained scars from the pain he'd inflicted despite the passage of time, and that some important things remained unsaid between them. Maybe he was right…maybe now that the worst of her anger had subsided, they needed to talk in order to move on unburdened. So, to her own amazement, she capitulated.

"All right." She sighed, and noticed some of the tension leaving his body. "I guess I could use a short break before the next round of torture, so let's get it over with. Just let me grab a snack and I'll meet you on the lawn."

Obviously relieved, Marcus gave her a small smile and squeezed her arm softly before letting it go.

"Thanks Lara," he said gently. "It means a lot to me."

"See you in five," she responded flatly, determined to ignore the butterflies that had started fluttering with his smile.

Chapter 22

Ten minutes later, she sat down cross-legged next to him on a sunny patch of grass, a tray of take-away coffees and pastries in hand. "Right-o, you've got the floor for as long as it takes us to finish these," she said, determined to keep the upper hand and to remain detached and unemotional, whatever transpired.

Marcus thanked her for the coffee and took a couple of sips of his before inhaling deeply.

"Okay, here goes. Just promise you'll hear me out before judging, okay?"

Lara thought for a minute, then nodded her assent.

"Great. Well, firstly, I should tell you outright that I'm a twenty-eight-year-old police officer, Lara. I'm not twenty-four. And my name's not Marcus—it's Michael…Michael Barker." He watched her intently as he paused to let his news sink in.

What? Lara just blinked, taking a moment to absorb his words, her mind reeling. But of *course* he would have used an assumed identity, she realized. Why hadn't the thought even crossed her naïve mind? She took a deep breath as he continued, already feeling surreal.

"So, for those and all the other lies I've had to tell you, I'm truly, truly sorry. That's the main thing I wanted you to hear; that I apologize for my deception, from the bottom of my heart."

She merely gave a small nod of acknowledgment, and he heaved a sigh of relief.

"Ten years ago, I started an undergraduate law degree in Sydney. But just when I'd finished second year, my father got shot by the dealer I told you about, and it really messed with my head. I left university and did some backpacking overseas, before realizing that what I really wanted to do was to follow in Dad's footsteps and join the police force.

"So I did the training and became a cop, working my way through the ranks until I joined the drug squad, and eventually ended up in the undercover unit about a year ago. I worked on three operations before this one, and didn't have any problems with it. In fact, it brought a whole new dimension to the job and made for a pretty interesting life, once I got used to the change. I was relatively young and single, so didn't care about being moved around, whereas some of the other guys find the separation from their usual environments pretty stressful. Then, when the job came up down here, I was the obvious choice for a role at this university, given that I'd already done half a law degree." He paused and stared thoughtfully into the middle distance, before taking a swig of his coffee and continuing.

"Our job was part of a big national operation, Lara. The guys heading up the syndicate are really bad news, and are involved in crimes way beyond drugs. So it was important work. And we had credible intelligence that one or more members of Burst were involved in the pushing—we just didn't know exactly who, when, or how. The plan was to gather enough evidence for an arrest, and then to offer a plea in exchange for them becoming state witnesses. Our main focus was on Charlie from the start, but we had to establish whether any of the others were involved, and could provide us with easier access to the suppliers. So Pete was definitely a person of interest in the earlier weeks.

"But two things happened that made this job very different for me. Firstly, I liked Pete immediately, which was an unexpected obstacle. The golden rule of undercover work is not to become emotionally attached to the subject of your investigation. As time went on, I became more and more convinced that he was on the outer, but I couldn't be completely sure whether my findings were being influenced by personal feelings. Keeping tabs on him became increasingly uncomfortable for me, and I can't tell you how ecstatic I was when his name was cleared. He's a really great guy, and I would have been honored to be his friend under different circumstances." With this admission, Michael shook his head, a cloud over his face. Then he looked at Lara, and his frown deepened further.

"The second thing that happened was you, of course..." Michael's voice cracked slightly on the last word, and he looked away and cleared his throat for a moment before continuing. "Obviously, a massive complication, destined to mess things up from the start..." At this point, Lara couldn't help raising a skeptical eyebrow, letting him know that she wasn't going to be led back down the garden path.

"Listen, I know you're probably going to question every word I say from this point," he deviated momentarily from his speech, adopting a more insistent tone in response to her body language, "because of what you *think* you know about me. So I won't go on and on about my feelings about you, Lara. I accept the stalemate we've reached on that point. But please allow me to make just a couple of admissions?"

She acknowledged his request and inclined her head once more with a sigh, while also pointing at her half-empty cup. *Round off your story then, if you must. But you'd better hurry.*

"Right, then." He took a deep breath and exhaled slowly before continuing. "Suffice it to say that I was attracted to you from the start. From the moment I first saw you in class, in fact. But I was absolutely, positively wrong to stay anywhere near you as soon as I realized you were in Pete's inner circle. There was a complete conflict of interest. I had a job to do, which involved adopting a false persona, not to mention the potential arrest of one of your good friends. It was definitely not the right way to start any sort of relationship. That's why I tried the cold shoulder routine in those early weeks, hoping that if you thought I was just some jerk, you'd keep your distance and we'd stay out of temptation's way.

"But, as you know, my self-control was pathetic. I did completely the wrong thing, and allowed things to progress between us. My resolve just kept weakening every time I saw you, until everything came to a head that day at the beach. That incredible day…" He shook his head, momentarily lost in the memory. "Anyway, that's my greatest regret, because it was inevitable that that contact was only going to end badly…an occupational hazard. It was just so inexcusable." He closed his eyes and swallowed before going on.

"So, Lara, please believe me when I say that I feel nothing but shame for the hurt and anger that I caused you and the others, however necessary the deception. The only thing I can offer in consolation is to assure you that a whole heap of pain came back my way too. I learnt a huge lesson from meeting you guys. I realized that I'm just not cut out for spying on people that I might actually like. I can handle the stress of living an alternate identity without blowing my cover, which a lot of people can't. But the guilt when things got personal and when I made such a mess of it all just about killed me. You might be happy to know that I've actually resigned from my undercover position. I'm back doing a desk job down here for the moment, before returning to uni as a full-time student for real next year. The plan is to get stuck into the legal side of crime prevention for a change." He took another long swig of his now-warm coffee.

"And…well, I guess that's it, in a nut shell," he finished with a shaky breath. "I can't believe I've managed to summarize ten years of my life in a matter of minutes! But I really appreciate the opportunity to catch up like this. It feels so good to be able to be honest with you, for once. Incredible, actually. I felt so rotten when you wouldn't let me explain myself after Charlie's arrest. I knew what you must've thought of me. Still think of me, probably."

Michael stopped talking and slowly put his cup back on the cardboard tray, his eyes fixed on Lara, while he waited for her to absorb all of his information. But after another minute of watching her as she sat lost in thought, he apparently couldn't help himself.

"Lara, you're killing me! Please, say something…anything. I need to know you've understood me…" he pleaded.

"Shh! I'm thinking. For God's sake, Marc…*Michael*, after months of keeping me in the dark about who you really are, you could try giving me a bit of time to take this all in!" She couldn't help herself, and he bowed his head, accepting her point. Finally, though, she spoke. "I've got questions."

"Of course. Shoot. Metaphorically speaking."

"Do you actually have a mother who's a bad cook and a sister who runs from doves?"

"Absolutely." He couldn't help but smile at the unexpected question. "I assure you that I stuck to the truth as much as I was possibly able to with you. Every word I told you about my life in Sydney and how I spend my free time was true. Well, except for the night owl act, that is…I'm usually in bed by ten and I despise clubbing."

"Especially when you miss surfing dates with nice girls the morning after the night before?" She couldn't help the barb.

"Ahh…yes. Especially then." He gave her a half-smile.

"Are you moving back to Sydney to continue your studies?" His eyes shifted away from her gaze.

"I'm not sure." She let that one go through to the keeper.

"Do you own a gun?"

"Obviously, Lara." Michael smiled. "It goes with the territory. I never had it on me when I was anywhere near you guys, though, if that's what's bothering you."

"Have you arrested people before?"

"Heaps of times. But each and every one of them deserved it, believe me."

"Have you ever shot anyone?"

"No, thank God. And I intend to keep it that way. I'm sticking to the 'pen is mightier than the sword' philosophy from now on."

"Where do you work?" She was having trouble picturing him in his real life.

"In the city."

"Do you wear a uniform?"

"Not as a drug squad analyst, no."

"Were you working there during your time with us?"

"Mostly not. You spend a lot of time on your own when you're undercover. My instructions were just to check in by phone at fixed intervals, unless vital information came to light, which of course it never did in Pete's case. I went to some team meetings from time to time though, to discuss strategy and then prepare for the bust. That's where I went a couple of times when I had to up and leave you, even though it was the last thing I wanted to do."

"Okay. Next. Were you monitoring Pete's friends, as well? Like Kate and me?"

Michael winced before replying. "We build research files on our subjects and, to a more limited extent, their relevant acquaintances. I'm sorry; it's a job requirement."

"'Operational Data'?"

"You got it."

"And you used listening devices?"

"Again, part of the job."

"Where?"

"Pete's share-house, as well as the other guys' places."

"So you didn't make any recordings of me? Like when we were alone together?" She had to check.

Michael raised his eyebrows. "What do you think? I'm not a complete prat, Lara."

"Yeah, well…just making sure." Time to hit him with the big guns.

"While we're on the subject of the two of us, whose idea was it for you to become 'romantically' involved with me in the first place—yours or 'the team's'? Were you following orders, or did you come up with that one all on your own?" Lara couldn't keep the bitterness out of her voice. Even now, it stung her to say the words, but she needed to know it all.

"What? No, Lara, you're way off base! Haven't you been listening? You've got to believe me..." He seemed genuinely flustered, running his hands through his hair in frustration. Then he stopped.

"Look, at the end of the day I guess you're going to see things your own way. All I can do is swear to you that *nobody* had *anything* to do with my 'decision' to become close to you, if that's what it was. It just happened, Lara."

Lara shuffled uncomfortably, sensing the distress behind his pleading words, unsure now what to believe. Her uncertainty was only exacerbated by the fact that this beautiful man was gazing unflinchingly at her with his piercing blue eyes.

"You should know some other things, too. I told my boss how things were between us, once it progressed to a certain stage. That was after we first went and saw Burst together, if you must know, when one of my partners—Angelica, the redhead—made it clear she knew how I was feeling and thoroughly disapproved. And I got an absolute caning for it. They nearly pulled me off the case, which I now think might have been for the best, all things considered. But, in the end, it was decided to keep me there as long as I backed off and kept things platonic. Which I was able to do, for a while. But the more I became convinced of Pete's innocence, the less I cared about protocol. Things between us felt like an unstoppable force, and I guess I'd started to let myself hope..." At that, he looked away from her for a few moments. "Anyway, my work was never placed in jeopardy," he finished in a rush.

Lara took a deep breath, her mind reeling at the picture he was painting. Was there any chance that Daniel could have been right? Could this more honest version of Michael, who walked a dangerous line in his job but was essentially a man of his word, really exist? The possibility sent her mind reeling—it was more than she could process. So she decided to maintain her silence for now, other than to ask one final burning question.

"All right, all right, I hear you, but I need to think about all of that. For now, though, I've just got one last question, and then I've got to get going."

"Fair enough." He sighed.

"You and me…exactly how much was real?" It was awkward, but she had to know.

Michael swallowed and closed his eyes before looking back at her and responding. "I thought that was obvious, from everything I've said to you, Lara. For me? Everything was real. Every bit."

Lara looked at him searchingly, before quietly replying. "Sorry, but after everything I've heard and seen, I can't buy that. I know you've said you had 'feelings' for me. But, Michael, our time together was defined by lies from the word go. So I'll ask you again…where did the truth stop and your quest for information start? And I'd appreciate a candid reply this time, if you can rustle one up. I'm a big girl."

Michael stared at her for a minute with a small frown, unsure how to proceed.

"Lara, I really don't know what else I can say. For God's sake, what do you want to hear? That I used you to fit in as a student and get close to Pete, and that every private word I said to you was to help me with my ulterior motive, while I enjoyed a bit of action on the side? Do you really think I needed to do all of that to get results with Pete? I'm a professional, Lara, and really, really good at my job." He shook his head, before reaching across and taking her hands in his, forcing her to look directly at him.

"I realize how much I've hurt you, and I can't blame you for being defensive, in the circumstances. But I beg you, please listen to me. *Listen*! Other than being forced to mask myself as a twenty-four-year-old student called Marcus who had a commitment phobia, every word I said to you on the personal front was the truth. Do you hear me, Lara? *Every word.* Every thought, every feeling, every admission. So, I get that you don't want a bar of me from here on in, and I can't blame you for that, but don't think worse of me than you have to. It's not fair to either of us." His cheeks were flushed with spots of color.

Lara didn't know what to think. She'd started this conversation with her brain already half fried after the lengthy morning exam. And she still had studying to do! She needed some time to digest everything he'd said—particularly his last declaration, which had sent an undeniable tingle down her spine. In many ways, today's conversation had made her feel like she was meeting a new person, but there was also a resurgence of the old comfort and longing triggered by his presence. It was totally confronting, not to mention bizarre.

"Okay, that's it, time's up. Enough," she said, retrieving her hands from his and holding them up in a sign of surrender. "Michael, I have to go. Quite honestly, I don't know what to think anymore. I do know that it's been—cathartic—to see you, and I'm glad we've had this talk, I guess. But to be frank, my head's spinning and I need to sort through everything you've said after I tackle my final exam. So I'd like to call it quits now, okay?" A pause.

"You mean, for good?" A longer pause.

"Probably. That is, I think so."

"I see."

"I'm glad someone does." They stared at each other.

"All right. Sure, if that's what you want," he replied with a look on his face that Lara couldn't quite work out. "I won't contact you again, Lara. I've said my piece. But, if you feel like it at any stage, will you call me? I'd really love to hear from you."

"Okay. Maybe," she agreed vaguely, unsure whether she ever would. What could it achieve, after all?

The two of them then rose together, and stood awkwardly for a few moments until Lara held out her right hand to shake his. At that, Michael started laughing at the absurdity of their position, the tension leaving his body.

"Anyone watching us would think we've just met for the first time and negotiated some sort of business transaction." He smiled, taking Lara's hand in both of his.

"And they'd be right, in a way." She smiled back, despite herself.

"But not in many others," he reminded her, keeping hold of her hand in one of his and tracing his fingertips lightly along her wrist with the other. The hairs on the back of Lara's neck rose at the contact.

"After all, if we were strangers, you wouldn't be wearing my gift…" He hooked his fingers beneath the charm bracelet he'd given her a lifetime ago. "I'm so glad you are…"

Lara cringed with embarrassment at his observation. Despite herself, she'd put the bracelet on for luck during the exams.

Then, letting go of her hand and standing upright once more, Michael dropped the intimate tone and resumed his more professional approach. "Anyway, thanks again for meeting with me, Lara, and for letting me have my say. It's been great to see you again, whatever happens from here." As they looked into each other's eyes for the last time, Lara tried to ignore her increased heart rate.

"Yeah, anyway. Take care out there, Marcus," she responded without thinking.

"Michael," he reminded her with an uncomfortable smile.

"Yeah, right," she replied deadpan, before turning with a wave and walking determinedly away. Michael.

Chapter 23

The labor law exam came and went the next day in a bit of a blur. It was a predictable paper, and Lara felt she'd done all right, despite not having spent as much time on the subject as her other three, and having remained distracted by the previous day's unexpected reunion. When the allocated time was up, she just laid her head on the desk and took some long, deep breaths. All she really cared about now was that the year of study had finally come to an end. After a whole lot of hard work and too many emotional ups and downs, she was completely exhausted.

Several hours later, after some downtime back in her apartment, Lara joined Pete and Kate for a fabulous dinner at a festive tapas bar in the city. They described their respective exam efforts in detail while downing shots and sangria and laughing more and more raucously as the night went on. The others were of course wide-eyed with curiosity and amazement upon hearing about all of Michael's declarations, and held completely contradictory views about how Lara should proceed. Kate was adamant that he was an untrustworthy rat who was probably still feeding her lies, and that he should be permanently avoided at all costs. Surprisingly, though, Pete felt that she should cut him some slack.

"It sounds like he only did what he had to do, Lara. We got caught up in the net, obviously, but it was only collateral damage, and it wasn't really Marc…err, Michael's fault. Other than getting hooked up with you, I suppose. But we've all done stupid things in the name of animal attraction…"

"Speak for yourself," Kate scoffed. "Some of us actually have the common decency to stick to the high road, even when temptation rears its ugly head."

"Well, what a boring world we'd live in if everybody was as sensible and smart as you are, Little Miss Perfect," Pete retorted, receiving a punch in the arm from both Kate and Lara for his efforts.

"Ouch! Cut it out, guys!" he continued. "All I'm saying is that I understand where the guy was coming from. He's not a monster, Lara. He's just flesh and blood like the rest of us, complete with the usual human failings."

"All right, all right, point taken," said Lara. "And I guess he at least had the decency to ensure we didn't become too *intimate*, if you know what I mean. Things could have been worse," she admitted.

"Don't make excuses for him, Lara. His ethical breach was still completely unacceptable," argued Kate.

"You're talking as a lawyer there, Katie, not as a woman," replied Pete. "If the police force can forgive Michael's actions, then maybe we should too."

"Not me." Kate shook her head furiously. "He'd better stay out of my way if he comes back here next year…"

"Enough, guys, enough," Lara interjected. "Let's close the book on the drama for now and have some fun. We've finished our second year of law school, remember? It's time to celebrate!" She held up her glass, determined to have a night free from heavy thoughts.

"I'll drink to that," agreed Pete, raising his glass too.

"You'll drink to anything," Kate snorted, before backing down. "All right, all right, truce. Here's cheers to my awesome study buddies. May your results and your summer breaks be outstanding!"

*

It only took a handful of days back at Anglesea for Lara's city life to retreat far into the shadows. She'd packed up her apartment for the break and forwarded her mail, before giving Daniel and Dan giant hugs and leaving the big smoke behind her. Goodbye, study and drama; hello, family and surf! The ocean sparkled a welcoming silver in the sunshine, and she was able to last longer out on the water than she had during the colder months. The days were glorious, and she and Gran cooked numerous barbeques in the back garden in the balmy evenings, listening to the currawongs and magpies making their final calls as the colors faded from the sky.

A couple of weeks into the break, she and an old school friend, Tess, decided to go on a brief "surfari" further along the coast before the real holiday crowd arrived. They packed up a few days' worth of clothes, some tinned and packaged food, and basic camping supplies, and set off at dawn on a Monday morning with their boards tied to the roof of Tess's old station wagon. Cranking up the radio and singing along to the classics on the local station as they drove, Lara felt younger and more liberated than she had since her teens. They spent aimless days incommunicado, trying out the various breaks along the Great Ocean Road, pulling in to whatever spot looked good at the time. Then, as dusk approached, they headed for the nearest camping ground for a shower, a cook-up, and some communal fireside conversation, before settling in for the night in sleeping bags on a mattress in the back of the car. It was a crowded and messy way to live, but they loved every minute of their freedom.

Returning home reluctantly at the end of the week, Lara became curious about Chief's whereabouts while she was rinsing her board and wetsuit out the back, and then even more confused when she realized that the house was uncharacteristically locked up. The instant she unlocked the back door and stepped inside with her gear, she knew for sure that nobody was home; the silence that greeted her was unmistakably one of absence. It was unlike her routine-obsessed grandmother to be out at this time of the day during the week. Where was she?

Shrugging to herself, Lara turned the lights on, put her dirty clothes in the wash, and took a long, hot shower before changing into a pair of jeans. It was only when she made her way into the kitchen to rustle up something to eat that she found the unexpected note stuck to the fridge.

Lara, your Gran has had a fall and hurt her hip. I've taken her into Geelong hospital. She'll be fine…Don't Panic. Bert.

So, of course, she panicked. The note, written by an old friend of her father's, was dated Wednesday—two whole days ago! Something had to be really wrong.

After standing in shock for a minute or two, Lara's head cleared and she grabbed the phone book and rang the hospital. She was put on hold a couple of times, before finally getting through to a ward supervisor, who confirmed that Gran had broken her hip and had already undergone surgery to insert a metal plate. The nurse patiently explained that she would remain an inpatient for a couple more days while she saw the physical therapist, but that she was resting comfortably with painkillers. Then she'd be mobile enough to go home and commence the recovery period, with some help from a physio, a nursing assistant and a walker. She was presently indisposed, but would be able to receive visitors later that evening.

As she hung up, Lara's fears were far from allayed. She closed her eyes tightly and took some deep breaths, feeling sick to her stomach that Gran had had to undergo surgery without her support. She wouldn't stop worrying until she laid eyes on the most important person in her life, and saw for herself that she was okay. So, after consulting the bus timetable, she packed up yet another bag with some supplies and walked briskly to the highway, ready to travel north this time.

Arriving in Geelong, she walked toward the familiar brick building near the center of town with trepidation…her family had already made more than enough trips there to last a lifetime.

Pushing such dark thoughts to the back of her mind, she entered the lobby and found her way to the right room. To her enormous relief, there was Gran, perched up in bed, looking paler and more fragile than usual, but as bright-eyed as ever. A smile creased her face and she held out her arms as her granddaughter nervously approached.

"Now, now, none of that, child. I'm absolutely fine, so stop your worrying right now!"

Lara fell wordlessly into Gran's arms, and soaked up the familiar smell and feel of her as they embraced. *Thank God, thank God*, was all she could think. She needed this woman to be all right, always.

"What happened, Gran?" she asked when she eventually pulled herself upright, still perched on the edge of the bed. "How did you fall?" Gran looked away for a minute, seemingly reluctant to answer.

"Oh, I just tripped out the back of the house. Broke my hip. Stupid of me, really. But it'll come good."

"But how did you do it?" Lara pressed, worried that Chief might have knocked her down.

"Hmm. Well, I toppled on the back steps, if you really want to know," Gran admitted somewhat tersely. The steps that she'd stubbornly refused to have fixed. A-ha.

"Oh Gran, no! Are you okay now? Is it very painful? Tell me about the surgery! When can you walk and come home?" Although Lara knew she was bombarding the poor patient with too many questions, she couldn't seem to help herself. She wanted all the answers and all the reassurances now, to make up for not being around when she was needed.

Gran held up her hands to slow the torrent, and asked Lara to find them both a cup of tea, so that they could talk their way through everything that had transpired. She assured her that the surgery had been a success, and that the prognosis was excellent, thanks to her fitness and general health. She'd be up and walking slowly again in only a couple of weeks, with some assistance, and her strength and movement would increase from then, provided she kept mobile and did her exercises. Hearing that, Lara was thankful that she was going to be home to help during the awkward weeks ahead. Maybe the timing hadn't been so bad after all.

Most surprisingly, Lara learned that Chief had actually come to Gran's rescue! He'd sat next to her and whined for some time after she'd fallen, wondering why she'd refused to move. Eventually though, the dog had run off and found Bert walking up the beach track. Barking up a storm and turning and trotting a few steps at a time toward the house before looking back, the dog had finally coaxed the old surfer to come and find Gran where she lay. Lara could hardly believe her ears. Lassie, eat your heart out!

"Where is the old devil, anyway?" she finally thought to ask. "I can't imagine Bert would've been happy to take him." Bert already had a grumpy old dog of his own, who undoubtedly wouldn't have taken kindly to sharing his home.

"Umm, no. I got another friend to take him for a couple of days," Gran said.

"Who?" Lara asked, puzzled by the vague response.

A long pause.

"Just a man I know. A very responsible one. A policeman, in fact."

Lara stared at her grandmother incredulously. "You've *got* to be kidding me…"

"I'm not, sorry," Gran responded sheepishly.

"Could you please explain to me *exactly* how that happened?" Lara couldn't keep the sharpness out of her tone.

Gran sighed. "He left me his number, Lara, that's all. That time he came to the house to see you. Said to call him if I ever needed anything. And, as it turned out, I needed help housing your dog, so I had Bert give him a buzz. End of story."

"But Gran, of all people, you had to call *him*? Surely there were other people…"

"Well, there weren't," Gran interrupted abruptly, her voice slightly raised. "I had to make a quick decision, Lara. My own friends are too old to look after that giant mutt; I would never ask that of them. And you and Tess were away, so I didn't know who else to call. I know you and Michael have had a falling out, but I like him, and most importantly, I knew he'd do the right thing by Chief. Which he did."

Lara felt duly chastised.

"I guess I should be grateful to him," she said quietly.

"Well, of course you should be," Gran retorted. "And while you're thanking him for dog-sitting, please also thank him for bringing in my clothes, and for staying and waiting here until I came out of surgery! I'd say he's been pretty amazing, actually."

Lara was speechless. Michael had been there for Gran, when she herself hadn't been around. She was having trouble registering that the person who'd brought her so much turmoil, and who she'd so recently farewelled, had landed squarely back into her universe. How could the two separate parts of her life have collided like this again?

With her startling news delivered, Gran changed the subject, and the two women talked for a while longer about the hospital food and the nurses. Lara soon noticed, however, that Gran was tiring, and stood to take her leave, promising to return the next day with some fresh clothes, a new novel, and a packet of butterscotch. Then, feeling sad at having to leave her grandmother in such a dreadful place, but thankful that she seemed to be doing as well as could be hoped in the circumstances, she made her way back to the bus stop, toward home.

Chapter 24

An hour or so later, Lara was back at Anglesea, with a hastily prepared dinner already finished and the lamps burning. After washing the dishes, she sat on the couch for quite some time, lost in thought. And as she analyzed her mess of feelings one layer at a time, the confusion slowly but surely cleared, until a single, startling realization remained: She had forgiven Michael, and she wanted to see him.

So, almost to her own amazement, Lara picked up the phone, her heart hammering in her chest.

"Hello?" He answered on the third ring.

"Hello."

She heard a sharp intake of breath.

"Lara." A statement, not a question. It seemed that he knew her voice as well as she knew his.

"Michael." A pause. "So, I hear you have something of mine."

"I do. And he's fine."

"It was good of you to take him."

"Well, it's all part of my cunning plan," he joked. "I had to get you to call somehow. I wasn't sure whether you would have, otherwise."

"I wasn't either, to be honest."

"It's good to hear your voice," he said softly, and the tiny hairs on the back of her neck rose.

"Hmm. Well, anyway, I hear that, in addition to taking in my dog, you've spent quite a bit of time with my grandmother."

"Ah. So she told you."

"She did."

"And…you're angry at me for interfering with your family? I know I promised that I wouldn't contact *you*, but we never said anything about—"

"I'm not angry, Michael," she interrupted him quietly.

Another pause.

"Okay then. Good."

"Actually, I was calling to say thank you, for all your kindness." She cleared her throat. "Gran really likes you, you know. Your being there during the surgery meant a lot to her."

"Well, you're welcome. It was no trouble at all. I really like her too, as you know, and I was worried. How's she doing today?"

"She's fine. As stoic as ever," Lara replied.

"I'm glad." Again, the silence grew between them. Thankfully, though, he pushed through their awkwardness.

"So…you want your hound back, I take it?"

"Whenever it suits."

"Of course." Michael sighed. "I'll bring him to you as soon as you want. But I'm going to miss him like crazy! He's been awesome company, and he makes me feel closer to you."

Lara became still.

"Thank you," she whispered again.

"My pleasure. Is that it, then?" he asked, his voice loaded.

"Yes," she replied. Then, "No. I'd like to see you," she finally managed, and heard an intake of breath at his end.

"I'm staying in Lorne. I can be with you in under an hour," he responded huskily.

"Sounds good," she managed to get out, before he rang off without another word.

*

It didn't take him an hour, rather, closer to half that. Lara walked to the front door when she heard his truck come tearing along the dirt road. Chief bounded out of the back almost before the car had come to a complete stop, and ran into her arms full of licks and gentle nudges before making his way into the kitchen to find his dinner.

"I think you might have just beaten the land speed record," Lara commented as Michael slammed the car door and walked deliberately up the path, his eyes locked onto hers the whole way. He looked relaxed, in cargo pants, sneakers, and an old cotton windcheater.

"Important business to attend to," he replied expressionlessly as he followed her through the front door.

Once inside, she led him to the living area, where he sat on the couch next to her with Chief at his feet. They sat in silence for a full minute, assessing each other openly, both trying to read the other's expressions and thoughts. Lara was also trying to quell the nervous flutter inside her that surfaced every time she was confronted with his stunningly handsome face.

"Wine?" she finally offered, pointing to the bottle of red and glasses on the table in front of them, which she'd placed there earlier with a plate of chocolate biscuits.

"Love some." He smiled, and the awkwardness was broken as she poured them both a glass.

"So did Chief really behave himself for you?" she asked.

"Perfectly. I took a couple of days off and have been staying at a mate's place in Lorne, which has a massive backyard. I reckon I threw his old tennis ball off the deck a thousand times while we were there! He sure does love that ball." Michael shook his head incredulously. "How was your surfing trip, anyway?"

Lara gave him an overview of the places she and Tess had been, and they shared a couple of laughs when she described some of the more colorful characters they'd met along the way.

"You sure do meet the best and worst of people when you're camping—the weird and the wonderful. A great way to take a true break from everything, though."

At that, Lara was reminded of what had been happening at home while she'd been away, and her smile fell. Michael seemed to notice her change in mood immediately, and quickly changed the subject.

"And tell me, how did your last exam go?"

"Who knows?" She shrugged, taking a sip of her drink. "I was kind of distracted."

"Oh. Sorry."

"So you should be," she retorted. "How did you go in all of yours?"

"Okay, I think. We'll see. As I said, it was a pretty big load, so my marks might have suffered a bit."

Lara nodded her head as she took a bite of a biscuit, and he watched her wordlessly for another long minute.

"I can't quite believe I'm back here," he said finally, shaking his head in bemusement. "I am *so* sorry about what's happened to Mrs. Lees, but I'm glad it's given me a reason to see you, all the same."

"Me too," she admitted.

"Why?" he asked directly.

So there was going to be no more small talk. Time to dig deep and show her hand, now that she'd decided how she felt.

"Because it's time for a change, don't you think?"

"I...I'm not sure exactly what you're saying..." he replied eventually, guarded. His body language was protective, and it dawned on Lara that, just as she was vulnerable to him, so he was to her. As beautiful as he was, he was not immune to pain. They had to look after *each other*, and it was high time to dispel any confusion or uncertainty between them. She took a deep, shaky breath. No ducking for cover now, she reminded herself.

"I'm saying that I want to believe in you, and I want us to give things a go," she said quietly. "That is, if you do."

His face was unreadable. He continued to gaze unblinkingly into her eyes, before answering her in a slow, measured tone.

"So, let me get this straight. Contrary to our last couple of discussions, you now think that we can place all the mess I created behind us and start afresh? Despite the lies, and our age difference, and the fact that you only learned my real name a couple of weeks ago?"

"Yes," she whispered.

"Why would you want to do that?"

"I think you know why." It was Lara's turn to pull protectively back, and to avert her eyes from his penetrating stare. But then he reached out and held her under the chin, lifting her head gently so that she was forced to confront him.

"I want to hear you say it," he said slowly and clearly, taking control of their discussion for the first time.

"That's not fair!" she protested. "I'm the one who called you, remember? As if I'm not taking enough of a risk…."

"Say it," he repeated insistently.

"Why should I?" she challenged him with a raised voice and flashing eyes.

"Why? Because you're not the only one taking a leap of faith here, you know. And reality needs to start right here, right now, Lara. After the *extremely* shaky start we've had, we've both got to commit to complete honesty every step of the way from this minute onwards. Otherwise, we'll never stop doubting each other. So…?" He raised his eyebrows, repeating his request again, wordlessly.

Lara closed her eyes, blanked her mind, and took the plunge he was demanding of her. "I want us to give things a go because I'm in love with you, Michael. I have been for months."

Silence, other than his light breathing over the sound of the distant waves. Lara took another steadying breath and forced herself to open her eyes and look at him, half-dreading what she might find. How many women had given themselves to him like this, and what was he going to do about it?

But when she saw his face, every muscle in her body relaxed instantaneously. Everything she needed to know and trust in was right there in front of her, his bright eyes glowing with relief and happiness. There was no other self-serving agenda.

"Thank you for your honesty, sweetheart," he said with a smile as he reached out to take one of her hands in his, his endearment making her feel like she was melting.

"And now it's my turn. I finally get the chance to say some things I've wanted to say for a long time. I can't believe it!" He pulled her hand up to his face and kissed her upturned palm before continuing.

"I'm pretty sure I fell for you at first sight, Lara, although I've never really believed in the phenomenon. It's what's inside that counts, after all. But from the very first day of uni I couldn't get this stunning brunette out of my mind, even though she gave me such an icy reception. And if not then, I was definitely smitten by the time you ran away from me in the law quad after literally dropping your bundle. Such crazy, uncomfortable behavior! And then, of course, I was a complete goner from the second I had the privilege of slow dancing with you at that stupid ball. I'll never forget the moment you finally relaxed in my arms…I wanted to keep you there forever. I didn't sleep a wink that night!"

Lara was following his words and memories with half her mind, but the other half was spinning, stunned that this perfect man was saying such incredible things about her.

"Next, well, you know my reaction when I saw you out dressed to kill the nights we saw Burst; although I'll admit there was a fair bit of lust in the mix on those occasions." Michael paused to tweak the end of Lara's nose playfully.

"But it was only through all of our talks that I finally understood just how much you meant to me." He reached up again and stroked her face lovingly, the depth of emotion in his eyes undeniable. "Then, once you finally showed me that you had the same sort of feelings that I did, I was simply unable to leave you alone, as you know, and decided just to let things take their course. But from the instant we got together on the beach—another memory that'll stay with me until the day I die—I realized just how explosive a closer relationship would be. I knew then that I had to put the brakes on, with the 'I've got too much going on for a proper relationship' routine. Half-baked, but necessary. I just couldn't let things progress further until you were certain…until you'd made a *fully informed* choice to be with me. The real me, that is.

"And now, unbelievably, you're now telling me you have! Which is more than I've dared to hope for." He smiled into her eyes. "So now I'm free to tell you all of it. That I love your mind and your body, your company, your relationship with the world. We're meant to be together, Lara, I'm sure of it. I want to be with you, and stay with you, for as long as you'll have me."

She simply stared at him, unable to breathe.

"I know that might sound completely over the top," he continued, as he reached out instinctively to comb her hair back with his fingers, "and I'll back off if you want me to. I'll never impose on your freedom, I promise. But I've got a few years on you, and I know my own mind. I know what I want, and that's *you*. Being apart from you over the last couple of months has been unbearable. I know we still have so much to learn about each other, you and I, but we've got a lifetime to do it. So, I'm yours from now on, for as long as I can make you happy. Forever, hopefully."

When he'd finished talking, he sat back and watched the emotions work their way across her face, allowing her time to absorb the enormity of his confession as he idly traced a finger back and forward across her wrist. And, taking in his words, Lara finally saw their union through Michael's clear and certain eyes, and allowed the last remnants of her insecurity to dissolve. He was real and solid, and he was hers, for keeps. Her life had changed unalterably, and beyond recognition. Now that she knew what to look for, his love for her, and the peace he'd found in declaring it, were completely apparent in his own expression, and her radiant smile revealed that she finally understood.

"You love me," she said slowly, trying the words on for size.

"I do," he agreed.

"You're perfect, and I'm not, but you love me anyway." She grinned.

"You have no idea what you're talking about, but yes, I love you anyway." He grinned back. "More than words can express."

Without taking her eyes off him, Lara put her arm along the back of the couch and leaned against it, enjoying relaxing in the warm room with a sigh and a blissful smile. Michael mirrored her position, before running his fingertips slowly up and down her arm.

"I don't want this feeling to end," she told him.

"Me neither," he agreed. "Hopefully it won't." His fingers were now brushing lightly up her neck and along her jawbone, and Lara's face moved instinctively toward him. Then she sat immobile, her eyes closed, and let Michael slowly explore the contours of her face with his feather-light touch. When he eventually reached her mouth, she allowed her lips to part slightly, and he stroked back and forward across them with his thumb, the pressure increasing when her breathing deepened. She surprised herself with a soft, involuntary groan, at which point she opened her eyes.

"That's not really fair, you know," she accused him.

"What precisely are we talking about?" he asked her distractedly, busy now playing with her hair again.

"It's not fair that you're so much more experienced with women than I am with men. You know exactly what to do all of the time, and I'm such a novice," she said with just a hint of embarrassment.

"That bothers you?" he asked, looking at her in surprise.

"It does a bit," she admitted.

"Well, it shouldn't. Firstly, if it makes any difference, I *like* that you're a novice. I'm hideously jealous of anyone who's been anywhere near you, like that guy at the ball." He frowned momentarily. "So I intend to make sure that you're never curious about other men again…

"Secondly, I haven't exactly slept with hundreds of women, Lara. I've had a couple of flings and two girlfriends—years ago now and they pale in comparison with you, believe me—and that's pretty much it. I've been really busy with my job and spending all my free time going bush over the last few years.

"And thirdly, for your information, you don't come across as a learner in the physical department, if that makes you feel any better. That's if memory serves correctly. Although, perhaps I need a refresher to be sure…"

But Lara barely registered Michael's words, because he'd leaned across while he was speaking, until their mouths were almost touching. She could feel his warm breath across her cheek, and was mesmerized by the assault on her senses. Then he moved his head to one side, his lips brushing against her jaw before he breathed into her ear, sending a shiver right through her body.

"Mmm, this is heaven," he murmured. She agreed wholeheartedly, her own lips grazing his cheek, and they stayed that way for a minute, simply breathing each other in. It was a familiar sensation—they'd been down this path before, after all. But it was very different too; the masks were off and their identities were on full show. To Lara, at least, it felt like their first time together all over again. Michael must have agreed, as he pulled back with an uncertain smile and a final stroke of her face.

"Are you ready for this?" he whispered.

"Let's see," she replied in kind, reaching her arms around his neck with an inviting smile. He leaned back in toward her in response.

"Come here, then," he murmured, before softly, softly placing his lips on hers. His kiss was warm and gentle, and so achingly sweet that it brought tears to Lara's eyes. It was unlike anything they'd shared before; the sense of urgency that had previously lain just beneath the surface was gone in the knowledge that today, time and commitment were on their side. This kiss was only about giving, without either of them taking a thing from the other…a sealing of the deal. Lara felt like her heart was going to burst out of her chest.

Then, after a while, it changed. Michael started kissing her more deeply, and Lara's body shuddered involuntarily as the air between them became electrically charged. His movements were laden with desire, and he was asking her permission to yield to the slow burn that had been building between them all evening and all semester, but which they'd kept at bay, until now. She responded to him with all the longing and passion that had been coursing through her body for hours, weeks, months. As one, their breathing quickened and they allowed their bodies to become entwined as they lay back on the couch, pressing against each other in their urgency to get closer still, revealing the full extent of their desire. At this, Michael groaned inadvertently, which only fuelled Lara's longing further, thrilling her with the understanding that he was as much at her mercy as she was at his. They were completely exposed to each other; reason had been replaced by animal instinct.

After some time, though, just as they were on the brink of being unable to stop themselves going further, Michael pulled gently, reluctantly, backwards. He observed Lara for a minute in silence while they allowed their hunger to subside and their breathing to quiet. There was a tacit understanding that, under Gran's roof, things had gone far enough.

Then, with a sigh, Lara shifted to settle back comfortably against his body, while he wrapped his strong arms around her and kissed her softly on her temple. She'd never felt so safe or nurtured in her life.

"I love you, Lara," Michael whispered, his voice loaded with unconcealed emotion. "This is more than I'd ever hoped for."

"I couldn't have put it better myself." She smiled in reply.

Chapter 25

Lara awoke the next morning to feel the sun streaming through the window onto her bed. Struggling to break through the fog of sleep, she stretched lazily as she listened to the familiar birdsong with a smile. Then, as her brain cleared, the events of the previous day came flooding back.

"Oh!" she said aloud, suddenly wide-awake. How could she have forgotten such a perfect night, even for a moment?

After their initial outpouring of emotion, she and Michael had stayed up talking for hours, sharing thoughts and feelings and stories, further revealing the tapestries of their lives with a new honesty that Lara had found enormously gratifying. Eventually, though, exhausted after everything that had happened, she'd had to call it a night, and had left Michael to a makeshift bed on the couch after one final, blissful kiss, when he'd pulled her against his hard, muscular body and they'd simply stood for an eternity, completely connected from head to toe.

"Sleep well, sweetheart. Sweet dreams," he'd whispered, before placing a feather-light kiss on her forehead and directing her gently toward her bedroom.

And she had done; and they had been…

As the memories resurfaced, Lara sat up abruptly and turned, and there he was: leaning against the doorframe, already dressed, a cup of coffee in one hand. As if greeting her in her bedroom on a Saturday morning was the most natural thing in the world! She couldn't help but catch her breath at the sight of his beauty in the morning sun. Even now, after everything they'd shared.

"Good morning." He smiled.

"You're actually here," she said.

"Sure am."

"For a second there, I thought I'd dreamt it."

"There's been a lot of that going around," he admitted.

"How long have you been standing there?" she asked a bit croakily, reaching up to try to rake her morning hair into shape, to no avail.

"Long enough. You're adorable when you're asleep; has anybody ever told you that?" Michael asked with a grin.

"Oh no," she groaned. "I wasn't snoring or dribbling, was I?"

"Hardly. Just giving the occasional sigh. It's been very peaceful to watch."

"I'm glad I've given you so much enjoyment," she responded with a hint of sarcasm, conscious of looking like a complete wreck next to his perfection.

"You look fine, don't worry," he assured her with a grin. "In fact, you have no idea what a privilege it is to see this side of you."

"Is that so?" she asked, somewhat mollified. "Well, you'll excuse me if I go and get rid of the morning breath, at any rate." She flung off the covers and put her feet on the floorboards. "Why are you so full of beans this morning, anyway? You drank as much wine as I did."

"Not full of beans—full of caffeine. Second cup." He pointed to his drink. "I was desperate."

"Couldn't sleep because of the couch?" she asked sympathetically as she rose.

"Couldn't sleep because of my housemate. Knowing that you were right in here all night was very…distracting," he corrected her with a knowing look.

"Oh," was all she could say, suddenly conscious of standing in front of him in only a thin cotton nighty.

"You said it!" He smiled, with one eyebrow subtly raised. "Maybe you should get into something, umm—less comfortable—while I rustle us up some breakfast." With that, he sauntered into the kitchen and commenced opening and shutting every cupboard and muttering to himself in his search for some cereal. Lara smiled as she changed into a pair of jeans and a shirt, and freshened up in the bathroom, noticing on her way that he'd already neatly packed up the couch-bed. Then, as she made to walk past him in the kitchen to prepare a fresh pot of coffee, he grabbed her unexpectedly and pulled her in close.

"Aahh, excuse me, but I think you've forgotten something, Ms. Lees." He nuzzled her neck, and goose bumps worked their way down her body in an instant.

"I have?" she asked. "Can't think what…"

"Then let me remind you," he growled, before kissing her hungrily and leaving her breathless. He grinned at her when they'd finished, utterly aware of the depth of her reaction to him. "Now, that's what I call a good morning kiss! I could get very used to this…"

So could Lara.

*

A little while later, Michael measured up the back steps in preparation for some much-needed maintenance, and Lara looked idly out across the garden and debated whether or not to stretch her legs before they left for Geelong to visit Gran again. All of a sudden, though, her thoughts were interrupted by Michael, who'd come up silently behind her and had wrapped his arms around her waist, pulling her insistently against him, while murmuring into her ear.

"No, I don't think a walk's in order right now," he said huskily, and she smiled at his mind reading. She allowed her body to relax under his expert touch, and rested her head back against him. He brushed her hair aside and started kissing her hairline. Then, without breaking contact, he turned her around in his arms, leaning her against the bench and molding the full length of his muscular body against her softer one, the perfect counterpart. His kiss was soft and deep, and it felt like heaven.

Then, as their yearning increased, Lara couldn't help herself. Breathlessly, she reached beneath Michael's t-shirt, her fingernails grazing against the hot skin of his back, exploring its hard contours. His breathing quickened in response and, for a time, their contact became entirely physical. But after a few minutes, Michael pulled abruptly away.

"God, Lara…just give me a minute, okay?" He leaned against the bench beside her as he fought for self-control, watching her closely but not quite touching. "Are you quite sure you haven't done all of this before?"

She shook her head. "My body just seems to know what it wants from you," she answered honestly.

"And that is…?"

"Everything," she said, but then hesitated. "Eventually."

Michael just grinned before replying. "There's no rush, girl. We've got a lifetime."

In the mood for more Crimson Romance? Check out *Catch a Falling Star* by Jessica Starre at *CrimsonRomance.com*.

www.ingramcontent.com/pod-product-compliance
Lightning Source LLC
Chambersburg PA
CBHW010638100726
47900CB00011B/2884